CHAS WILLIAMSON

Paradise Series: Book Four

STRANDED
in Paradise

Print ISBN: 978-1-64649-104-9

eBook ISBN: 978-1-64649-105-6

 Year of the Book
135 Glen Avenue
Glen Rock, PA 17327

Dedication

Stranded in Paradise has been a partial trip down memory lane for me. My heroine Aubrey finds herself in a strange and unique setting with people so different than she'd ever met. A long time ago, I was blessed to meet this special girl, like none other I'd ever encountered. A woman who said what she meant and meant what she said. One who wore her heart on her sleeve. The one who loved me for all my flaws and didn't want to change me; she only wanted to share and enjoy a life with me.

My existence was forever (and wonderfully) transformed by her. For you see, in this woman's arms, I found all I would ever need. Together, we've blazed the trail of life and found true happiness. We've mastered the waves life sent our way, clinging to our love through the rip currents and rogue waves we faced.

Janet, as we stand hand in hand, preparing to meet eternity, know this one thing. Your love has taken me to Paradise and I look forward to sharing eternity with you there. This book is dedicated to you.

When the grass has withered,
And the stars all burn out,
When the waves no longer stir,
And time is but a memory,
Our love will remain, true, deep, eternal.

Acknowledgments

To God, for blessing me beyond my wildest dreams. For sending these characters into my mind and for allowing me to see stories and adventures everywhere I go.

To my best friend, for always believing and loving me. Without you, I would be nothing. You are my world and because of you, I'm living happily ever after.

To Demi, for your guidance, direction and encouragement.

To my beta readers, Connie, Mary, Sarah and Janet for your suggestions, help and tweaks to make my words better.

To Fran Tarkenton, Alan Page, Boog Powell, John Havlicek and Bobby Orr, the heroes of my youth, for giving me hope until I met the real heroes in my life.

To every single naysayer I've ever met, for your words backfired and made me even more determined to achieve my dreams.

Prelude

Mid-April

T he stench of the subway was stifling this morning. Aubrey Stettinger clamped the napkin over her muffin, as if that would keep the odors from affecting the taste. The bitter essence of her black coffee seemed to help, calming her nerves. *Never meant to spend the night.* She'd fallen asleep at her friend's house. After hours of rehearsing yet another script so she could audition. Rachel was a high school drama teacher, excellent coach and Aubrey's closest friend.

The subway train pulled into the station. Aubrey yanked the strap on her backpack a little tighter and climbed aboard. The car was pretty full, but she located a seat and quickly scanned the passengers. Most seemed to be commuters bound for Wall Street.

One young man did catch her eye. Tall, cute, tan. Self-confidence flowed out of every pore. He was dressed in nice jeans and a golf shirt with the name of a university she didn't recognize emblazoned on the left breast, Millersville. The man was engaged in soft conversation with a tall and big-boned woman with short red hair. *Oh well...*

Aubrey slipped the wrapper aside and nibbled on her cinnamon muffin. She had no sooner moved the food from her lips when the door between the cars flew open. A filthy, wild-haired man stumbled through the opening, dragging a large black garbage bag along with him. *Poor man, probably everything he owns is in that sack.* The man's gaze suddenly fell on Aubrey. Despite looking away quickly, she detected his steady movement as he shuffled until he stood in front of her.

The overpowering stench of dried urine permeated the train car. Without a word, the man grabbed the muffin from her hand and shoved most of it in his mouth. When he spoke, crumbs flew out, covering her legs. "Gimme your drink!"

Aubrey handed him the cup, standing so she could walk away from the scary guy. The man then seized her backpack and yanked it so hard she landed on her knees.

He tried to rip it away from her. "Let go! Mine now." Before she could say a word, he kicked her arm with his foot.

Unwillingly, Aubrey released it. He plopped down, cradling her bag in his arms as he sat in the seat she'd previously occupied.

No, no. This can't be happening. "Please give that back to me. You can have the coffee and food, but I need my backpack."

"Nope. Get away from me."

When Aubrey reached for her bag, he threw the brew at her. She lunged to the side, falling into the lap of one of the Wall Streeters, as the hot liquid narrowly missed her. The well-dressed man shoved her to the floor, right into the puddle of coffee.

The fire in the crazy man's eyes was scary.

Now what do I do?

"Excuse me, sir. I believe you have something that belongs to the lady. Kindly hand it back to her." Aubrey turned to find the man wearing the Millersville shirt standing next to her.

"Get lost, idiot."

The train was starting to slow for the next station.

The stranger stepped forward, grasped the homeless man's hand and twisted it until the smelly man was on his knees. Her hero's voice was calm. "Please, sir. I'm trying to be nice, but I won't ask a second time. Hand the bag to the lady, now. I don't want to hurt you, but I will if I need to."

The homeless man screamed and howled, but then threw Aubrey's shoulder bag at her.

The tall man released the villain and touched Aubrey's shoulder. "You alright?"

She was shaking from head to toe. "Th-thank you."

Her rescuer helped her to her feet, then nodded. "Everything's fine. Take my seat, over there. I'll keep an eye on him, and I guarantee he won't bother you, ever again."

The rail car came to a sudden stop. The crazy man scrambled to his feet and lunged out the door. Aubrey's new friend grabbed the garbage bag and chucked it after him just as the train doors started to close.

Aubrey plopped down next to the Millersville man's companion. The red-haired woman immediately jumped up, moving until she stood behind Aubrey's rescuer. The expression on the other lady's face seemed to be a mixture of anger and disgust, as if a filthy animal had tried to touch her.

But the man shot Aubrey a warm smile. "Are you okay?"

Aubrey realized her hands were trembling. "Yes. Thanks again." Suddenly, there was so much more Aubrey wanted to say to the stranger with the bright blue eyes. Like, *"Who are you?"* But when she opened her mouth, nothing came out.

***

Connor Lapp had noticed the pretty girl when she entered the rail car. Slender and pale, her beautiful auburn hair was curly and ended well below her shoulders. But the thing that he really noticed, what made him shaky inside, was those deep brown eyes. The way they curved as she surveyed her surroundings had him feeling so, so, so suddenly... alive. *Wow. Wonder if she realizes how stunning she is.*

"How long will it take you?"

He drew his gaze from the nameless female and focused on Marci, his girlfriend. Her green eyes were studying him with intensity. *As always.* "Will what take?"

"Whatever you have to do with your *sister*."

He shifted his body to face Marci. *It was a mistake, bringing you on a business trip.* "Leslie wants me to check out the work one of our sub-

4

contractors did, then she and I are meeting with some prospective clients. I should be done by two..."

The redhead shot him a scowl. "Fine. I'll head uptown to do some shopping. Meet me at Tiffany's at two, sharp."

"Tiffany's?"

"That's what I said."

"I'll try."

"No. Be there and wear something other than that stupid *Millersville* shirt."

"What have you got against the 'Ville?"

Marci placed her hands on her hips. "As I've told you before, I do not like it when you wear that type of shirt. It makes you look like a walking billboard."

Connor shook his head and hoisted his computer bag. "Brought a change of clothes along, just for you."

"While we're in the city..."

The gruff voice interrupted his concentration. "Gimme your drink!"

Connor watched the drama unfold. He glanced around the car. Eyes straight ahead, not a single person was going to do anything to help the girl. When the man tried to throw coffee on the curly-headed woman, Connor had enough. *Not on my watch.* He took action, making sure her bag was returned and then directing her to his seat. Connor stared the attacker down and must have scared him, because the man fled the train at the first opportunity, leaving his belongings. *He might need this.* Connor threw the man's bag after him.

He then turned to check on the girl. She was shivering and looked as if she was trying not to cry.

Marci stood up and moved behind him. He easily read his girlfriend's expression. *She's mad at me. Go figure.* But the big, soft eyes of the stranger questioned him. No, not questioned him... *touched* him, somewhere deep inside. And Connor knew in that instant he'd never be the same. Lacking anything witty to say, he simply asked, "Are you okay?"

The girl brushed her bangs from her eyes with shaking hands. And she thanked him, but it felt as if she was going to say something else. *Please talk to me.* Suddenly, Connor willed time to stop so he could find out her name, her thoughts, who she was, what her preferred color was, favorite type of music... everything. But the train rolled to a stop and the doors slid open. Marci grabbed his arm. "Let's get out of here."

Something squeezed his heart. "Be right there." The girl had stood, but was watching him keenly. Reaching into his pocket, Connor grabbed some bills. He offered them to the girl. "I know the man took your food and drink. Use this and get some more, on me."

Those expressive eyes were making him woozy, as if he were drunk. "I couldn't, but thank you." She offered him her hand.

When they touched, a sensation flashed all over his body. His vision drew her in until he could almost see his image reflected in her eyes. "It's been my pleasure. I, uh, hope the rest of your day is... is... really special." A smile slowly covered her face, but it started in her eyes. She still didn't speak, so he filled the silence. "Nice to have met you. Bye, now."

Connor made sure the bills remained in her hands when he withdrew from her. He backed away, wishing he could get to know her or at least find out her name.

Marci's icy words broke the spell. "Are you coming, Romeo?"

"Yes, yes."

He shot a glance at his girlfriend. Her jaw was clenched, lips set in a fine white line and the words were like steam escaping a leaking pipe. "Always have to be the hero, don't you?"

Connor reached for Marci's hand, but she yanked hers away. "There was no one else to help her."

She stopped and pivoted until she faced him. "No one to help the poor, little, defenseless damsel in distress. Except for the honorable Connor Lapp. Know what? I think she deserved what she got."

He couldn't believe the anger in his woman's eyes. "What?"

"Did you see the holes in her filthy jeans? How her hair was unkempt? And talk about ugly... have you ever seen a girl with such a high forehead? Probably going bald from taking drugs or something, but you, the white knight, you just had to come to her rescue, didn't you?"

Why was Marci so angry? *I didn't think the girl was ugly at all. She's gorgeous. Very beautiful curls and those eyes...* But Marci didn't like her. Why? It hit him. *Marci's jealous.* That explained it. Okay, he needed to diffuse her anger immediately or he'd hear about it for days. A sly thought surfaced in his mind. "Actually, I was thinking about what I would do if that had been you, being attacked by a madman. That's why I acted that way. In my heart, it wasn't her, but you, Marci. It was you I was protecting."

Marci's expression changed. A smile tugged at the corners of her mouth, finally pulling her lips along. She reached down and kissed him. "That's better. Don't you ever forget you love me."

Connor kissed her in return. "How could I?" *You remind me all the time.*

Marci reached for his hand and they walked toward the exit. At the stair landing, he shot one last look, hoping to catch a glimpse of the girl. She was standing where he'd left her, but her eyes were on him. She raised her hand in farewell. *I wish...* Connor nodded, regretting not even knowing her name. *Probably better that way.*

Chapter 1

Mid-August

Aubrey returned the cell to the pocket of her waitress apron. The entire building seemed to be shaking. *They picked me!* She'd finally made it! Even though it wasn't the lead, it was a strong supporting role. *My chance to finally make it big on Broadway. We did it, Mama.* It took all of Aubrey's concentration to attend to her customers. Her feet didn't seem to touch the floor, even when the shift ended.

Aubrey speed dialed her friend's number. The voice on the other end of the line sounded tired. "Hey, Aubrey. What's up?"

"Rach. Are you sitting down?"

Stalled silence. "Why?"

"I-I, uh, I got the role."

Aubrey had to pull the phone away from her ear. "No way! I'm so, so proud of you. When?"

"It opens in two months. Rehearsals begin next week." Her phone vibrated. *Piotr.* "Can I call you right back? My boyfriend's calling."

"Come over. We'll celebrate. I'll throw a bottle of wine in the freezer to get it cold. Sound good?"

Aubrey had to stop to keep from walking into the back of the man in front of her when the light changed. "Rachel, you're the best. I'll be at your place as soon as I can. Thank you for everything."

"Best friends, Abs, best friends. Tell Piotr I said hello."

Aubrey touched her phone and connected with the second call. "Hey babe, do I have news for you!"

"Me, too. I need to go first," he said.

Something about his voice troubled her. "What's wrong?"

"Don't know how to say this... I'm not going to make our breakfast date tomorrow."

"Okay. Want to do it Sunday?" The light was ready to change. In a hurry to make it to Rachel's, she stepped through the crowd to beat the rush.

"That's not going to work, either."

"Why not?"

Piotr sighed. "I decided to return home."

Aubrey stopped in mid-stride. "Home? You mean like back to Poland? Why?"

Before he had a chance to respond, a screeching noise to her left drew her attention. Her mouth went dry as the rapidly expanding vision of the speeding truck grew before her eyes. Without enough time to try and evade, Aubrey dropped her phone and threw her hands out in front of her.

The action probably prevented a broken nose, but didn't stop her painful landing onto the street. The pain was excruciating.

A crowd formed around her. Everything was starting to become confusing. A clown was standing over her, a cop next to him. Both of their mouths were moving, but none of it made sense.

Aubrey's eyes focused on a solitary drop of rain. Her first glimpse of it was as a twinkling sparkle of light, maybe four stories above. It grew larger and larger until it struck, dead between the eyes.

Along with the drop of moisture, came total darkness.

***

Connor stretched and lunged, but missed the streaking tennis ball. His friend, Joe Rohrer, laughed. "I do believe that was match point. Did you let me win again?" Joe walked to the net and extended his hand.

Connor wiped the sweat from his eyes and shook hands with his friend. *He loves to show me up.* "Yeah, you got it. If I don't let you win every once in a while, you might want to quit on me." *Fifth time in a row. I'm on the string for lunch, again.* "Let's head in."

The pair strolled into the clubhouse, toward the restaurant. "Since you're buying, I'm in the mood for a broiled crab cake sandwich. They're really good here. Want one?" Joe was smiling.

"That sounds good, but as a doctor, I'm sure you remember that I'm allergic to shellfish. I'll get my standard, a bacon cheeseburger." They found their usual table and gave their orders to a pretty waitress, late teens or maybe twenty. Connor caught her checking out his friend. "Hmm. Me thinks the young lass liked what she saw."

Joe cast a dismissive glance at the retreating figure, shook his head and turned to Connor. "Why wouldn't she? Handsome man like me, in the prime of life." Joe stifled a chuckle. "And no one else nearby that's even close enough to perfection to make a comparison to. But alas, she's too young." Rohrer raised his eyebrows. "In reality, Connor, she only glanced at me because you've got 'the look'."

"What look?"

"You know. The look of a man who's taken. And you wear it on your face like a woman wears an engagement ring. By the way, how's Marci?"

Connor tried to hide his smile. "Well. Do I really have that look?"

"You betcha." Joe studied him closely. "I'm worried about you, Connor. Is Marci the one for you, really?"

Connor sucked some soda through his straw. "She thinks so."

Joe laughed. "And what does Connor Lapp think?"

How do I answer? "Sometimes I believe I am, but then other times..." He allowed his voice to trail away.

"Other times?"

Connor wiped his mouth with a napkin. "Sometimes, the relationship just seems all one-sided, that's all."

"Really? Thought you were in love with her."

"She says that, and I am, really I am, but..."

Joe shook his head. "Man, this is like removing an impaction. Speak freely, son. You're among friends."

"Joe, after all this time, she still hasn't told me she loves me."

"What?"

"And yet, she's been dropping hints about wanting an engagement ring. When we were in New York a couple of months ago, she dragged me to Tiffany's and looked at just about every ring they had."

"Tiffany's? Wow, she's going for the jugular. And what do you think? Ready to make that kind of commitment?"

Connor looked away. "We've been dating three years and I should be, but sometimes it feels... it feels like there's something missing. She has such a negative attitude about every other woman I've known, including Leslie."

"Ah. She doesn't like your sister. Why?"

Connor waited while the waitress dropped off their lunch. He noted the teen brought Rohrer another drink, but forgot Connor's, even though his glass was empty and Joe's first one sat there untouched. "She hates the fact that I live with and work for my sister. Marci wants me to find another job."

"And what does Connor want?"

Connor shot him a disgusted look. "Don't speak about me in third person. I'm sitting right here, dude."

Joe took a bite of his crab cake, but still spoke. "Okay. What do you want?"

"I like what I'm doing. I'll admit, engineering interior design projects isn't all that challenging, but Leslie and I are a great team and I'm having fun."

"So now what?"

"I don't know." It was time to change the conversation. "So what about you, Doctor Joseph L. Rohrer? How's your love life?"

His friend was suddenly interested in the ketchup bottle. "Non-existent. Still messed up over Tara."

Connor knew all about Joe's attraction to Tara, who was a nurse practitioner. His friend fell in love with her years ago when they were both taking their medical training, but she was in a long-term relationship. Then, when Tara and her boyfriend broke up temporarily, she and Joe had gotten together. "You really loved her."

"Um-hmm. Thought she was the one, but I guess that wasn't in the plans." Joe had sensed Tara still had feelings for her ex. "I had to know. That's why I sent her back to him." His friend shook his head and sighed. "I believed it would bring her closure and she'd come running back to me. But what happened? She married him." Rohrer ran a hand through his hair before looking directly at Connor. "Did I tell you I ran into Tara last week? She's expecting, again."

"Sorry. Joe, God has a plan for each and every one of us. Just because He closed that door doesn't mean He won't open the window to love again." Connor could see the expression of disappointment on his friend's face. "Hey, I've got an idea. Leslie's single. Nicest girl I know and she's even kind of pretty, in dim light."

Rohrer finally laughed, hard. *Good. He needs some humor.* The man finally got it out. "And you wonder why Marci doesn't like your sister. Sounds like you have a sis crush." His friend's face turned serious. "Do you know why I've never asked Leslie out?"

A tingle crossed Connor's shoulders. "Why?"

The sudden grin signified more teasing to follow. "If I married her, I'd be stuck with you as a brother-in-law."

They were silent for a while. "I'm going to invite you to our Labor Day picnic. And maybe you should open your eyes. My sis is kinda cool. And it could be you'll find your future there."

Joe studied his drink for a while, then nodded. "Okay. Maybe. Guess we'll see what God has planned."

Connor nodded. *Yes, we will.*

***

Aubrey sat up in the hospital bed when Rachel entered. There was a pretty brunette with her. "Hey Aubrey, how are you feeling?"

Like crap. "Okay, I guess." Aubrey shook her head. "Actually, I hurt all over and I'll admit, I'm more than a little depressed." She took a deep breath. "Thanks for coming. Who's your friend?"

The brunette offered her hand. "I'm Leslie Lapp. Rachel and I were sorority sisters at Alvernia. She told me about your accident. Sorry."

Stinks to be me. "It happened at such an inopportune time. I'd just landed a role on Broadway, but now... And to top it off, a *clown* was driving the truck that hit me."

Rachel patted Aubrey's arm. "The clown part was kind of ironic, but I feel so bad about the whole thing."

Aubrey continued. "Now, I not only lost that role, but I've got to figure out what to do. Can't stay at the apartment with the other girls, since there are no elevators to my floor. And I'm *not* going back to Minnesota."

Rachel's eyes were funny, as if she were excited about something. "So the social worker told you the only option is a rehab hospital?"

Aubrey clamped her lips and exhaled sharply. "That's right and I have no idea how I'll afford that."

Her best friend was now smiling. "The other guy's insurance will handle it, but I think there's another choice you haven't considered."

Aubrey was confused by the look on Rachel's face. "Such as?"

Leslie placed her hand over Aubrey's. "Ever been to Lancaster County?"

Lancaster? "No, where's that?"

"PA. Right in the heart of Pennsylvania Dutch Country, you know, where the Amish live. What would you think about going there to recuperate?"

Aubrey glanced at Rachel, whose smile was now a mile wide. "Do they have a rehab hospital there?"

Leslie shrugged. "They do, I guess, but I have a different suggestion."

Aubrey studied the woman. Her blue eyes and facial features reminded her of someone. *Seems like I should know you.* But she couldn't immediately identify who Leslie reminded her of. "Okay?"

"Stay with us. My house is wheelchair friendly. Had it modified for my grandmother when she couldn't climb stairs, before she passed away. Ramps, shower, kitchen, bed. All set up... and you know, there's no one using her old bedroom. Why don't you come and stay with us?"

Aubrey shivered, like she did when watching a horror movie. *This is weird.* "I-I don't even know you. And who is 'us'?"

Leslie's laugh was comforting. "My brother lives with me. And my mother is always there, keeping us in line. Nice, comfortable and quiet. A great place for you to heal."

"Wh-why would you offer to do that?"

Leslie took Rachel's hand. "Rachel spoke highly of you and asked if I would mind. And I don't. Actually, I'd be honored. Any friend of Rachel's is a friend of mine."

Hmm. *There's always a catch.* "How much would it cost? I don't have a whole lot of money."

Leslie now stood next to Aubrey. "Where I come from, friends help each other without any expectation of being paid."

This is too good to be true. "I don't think I could do that." There had to be some drawback.

Leslie frowned. "Why not?"

"'C-cause I, I won't accept charity."

The brown-haired woman rubbed her own chin and looked toward the horizon. "My brother has been pestering me for an assistant to help him."

"Help him do what?"

"We do interior design. It's just the two of us." Leslie laughed. "My brother complains I'm the boss and he's stuck doing all the grunt work. He really does need help staying organized. Want to come work for the Lapp Interior Design Team? That is, in between rest and recuperation."

Aubrey was shaking her head. Rachel cleared her throat. "If it doesn't work out, you could always head to the rehab hospital."

Not much of a choice. She'd seen the inside of too many of the hospitals her step-father took her to. Maybe a change of scenery wouldn't be so bad. "You promise?"

Rachel made an 'X' across her chest. "I'll talk to you every day and if you're not happy, I'll personally come get you."

Aubrey studied her best friend's eyes. Rachel smiled and nodded. Aubrey turned to Leslie and extended her hand. "I g-guess we have a deal... boss."

Chapter 2

T he rhythmic cadence of the tires on the expansion joints rocked Aubrey to sleep soon after the vehicle entered the New Jersey Turnpike. Recollections of her last conversation with Piotr taunted her.

"I still don't understand why you've decided to return to Poland."

He sighed. "I need to inform you of something, Aubrey."

A chill ran across her shoulders. "Inform me? Of what?"

Piotr hesitated. "I'm married. My wife is pregnant."

The shock almost knocked her out of the hospital bed. "Y-you're m-married? How long has this, I mean, have you been married?"

"Three years. But I want to explain something."

Her vision tinged with red. "Three years? During the five months we dated, seriously, I might add, you were married? At what point did you decide it wasn't really important to tell me?"

"Our marriage was over, and still is. Natalia emailed to tell me she is with child. And it is mine. This is the only honorable thing to do."

Aubrey struggled not to cry. "All this time you used me. None of it was real, was it?"

His loud sigh echoed through her brain. "My little Aubrey, it is real. I love you, not her. I'll put her ring back on my finger, long enough to give the child a name. Then, I'm coming back to you."

At that point, Aubrey disconnected, unfriended him on Facebook and blocked his number. Yet his dark eyes haunted her dreams. *What a jerk. How could I ever have loved him?*

"You awake back there?"

Aubrey shook her head to drive away the bad memory. She glanced out the window. They were sitting at a stoplight. A horse-drawn buggy pulled up next to the vehicle. Three children, two girls wearing bonnets and a small boy with a straw hat, were sitting on the back of the open-sided buggy. They were gazing into Leslie's Suburban. Aubrey waved, but they either didn't see or ignored her as the buggy turned onto a side road.

"Hello. Young lady in the back seat. Did you get a good nap?"

Aubrey glanced at the rearview mirror. Leslie's smile reflected in the glass. A horrible odor filled the vehicle. "What in the world is that smell?"

Leslie laughed. "Welcome to Lancaster County. Oh, the fragrances you'll encounter here... Better get used to it. Most of it comes from the Amish farms."

"Where are we?"

"On the outskirts of Lancaster. We'll be home in about ten minutes. Just spoke to Mimes. She has lunch waiting on us."

"Mimes? Who's that?"

Leslie's laugh reminded her of something, but she couldn't place it exactly. "That's my mom, but since her granddaughter came along, she refers to herself as Mimes." It came back to Aubrey, the memory. Of a happier time when her own mother lived with her in the Midwest. Laughing and splashing as they cooled off in the creek.

Aubrey's mind wandered during the rest of the drive, while her eyes took in the rural scenery. *So different than Minnesota. There are actually people here.* She counted eleven buggies before Leslie pulled into the driveway of a large yellow house with green shutters. It looked like an old farmhouse, with a big single-story addition tacked on. A wheelchair ramp dominated the yard before terminating onto a large wraparound porch. An older woman with gray-streaked dark hair and a girl of maybe seven or eight walked to meet them.

Leslie slapped the transmission into park and turned off the engine. "Look, here's our welcoming committee."

Leslie popped the rear gate and unloaded the wheelchair before opening Aubrey's door and helping Aubrey slip into the chair.

The older woman extended her hand to Aubrey. "Hi. My name's Mary, but you can call me Mimes. Everyone does."

Aubrey could sense they were trying to be friendly, but she was uncomfortable. *Hope I didn't make a mistake coming here.* The girl was dancing around. "So you're Aubrey? I'm Greiston, but you can call me Grey. Happy to meet you." The girl's hand was warm and wiggly when she grabbed Aubrey's.

Mimes pushed the chair up the ramp while Greiston and Leslie carried in Aubrey's duffle bags. The inside of the house was well decorated and homey. The reception she'd received and the charming interior calmed her nerves. Well, maybe a little. Leslie gave her a tour before leaving Aubrey alone in a large bathroom. It was set up for a wheelchair.

After Aubrey had freshened up, she swung the door open. The delectable scents of cooked chicken and homemade bread were waiting and wound their way to Aubrey. *Smells luscious.*

Mimes smiled as she placed a large bowl of soup on the table. "I made a special meal to welcome you. It's a Lancaster County favorite, chicken corn soup, to help you feel better. We're so glad you're here. Hope you're hungry."

I'm famished. "This is, uh, really nice, but you didn't have to go to any trouble."

"Nonsense, it was no trouble at all." Mimes turned to the girl. "Grey, would you please say grace?"

Aubrey witnessed the three ladies clasp their hands and bow their heads. She followed suit, though it wasn't her normal custom. "Dear God, thank You for the food, and for Mommy and Daddy and Mimes and Aunt Leslie and Uncle Connie and my new friend, Aubrey. Help her get better quick, but not too soon. I want to have time to play with her."

The sincerity of the girl's words touched Aubrey, but one comment struck her as odd. "That was a nice prayer, Grey. But didn't you mean Aunt Connie?"

The girl shook her head as she slurped a mouthful of soup. "Nope. He's Uncle Connie."

Aubrey turned to Leslie, who had merriment in her eyes. "Grey's talking about my brother, Connor. We all call him Connie, mainly to tease, but also as a term of endearment. Connor is my younger brother."

"I see."

"You'll get to meet him tonight. He drove to Atlantic City yesterday. We've got a hotel project there and he went to check on the contractors."

"Uh, okay."

Mimes offered her a basket of bread and a tub of real butter. "My son is very nice. Leslie told me you'll be giving him a hand with things... after you rest a while first. That's really nice. Connie's super busy."

Is that why they brought me here, to be his helper... or slave? Aubrey was quiet as they ate. Grey told her all about school and her mommy. The little girl stuffed a piece of bread in her mouth. "Mommy and Daddy have different houses. Maybe you'll meet my daddy. I really like my daddy. He's funny."

A slight frown covered Leslie's face. "Lisa and Dirk are divorced. Grey stays with us occasionally, usually after school, though it seems to be on a more frequent basis lately. Lisa works in Harrisburg. Sometimes Dirk picks up Grey, on his days and weekends."

Grey continued her soliloquy during the meal. Though she offered, Mimes wouldn't let Aubrey help clean up after the meal. Aubrey rolled herself onto the porch, where it was warm. A pleasant and fragrant wind lulled her to the edge of slumber. She was still confused as to why Leslie had eagerly brought her here. *People don't just do nice things for free.* New Yorkers had taught her that, in ways she'd never forget. The twittering calls of the birds and the warmth of the sun finished the job.

The sound of tires on gravel woke her. For a second, Aubrey forgot where she was. She was in the process of getting her bearings when a man climbed out of a pickup and started up the ramp.

Aubrey's heart stuck in her throat when she got a good look at him. *How can this be possible?* His hair was shorter, but she hadn't forgotten his face. The one that filled her dreams each night.

The man stopped and his mouth fell open. He shook his head and took a second look at her. While his face was red, Aubrey knew hers must be even more scarlet. He pointed at her and a wide smile took hold. "Where'd you come from?" He stepped closer. "I can't believe this. It's you, really you. The pretty girl from the subway." He offered his hand. "Are you the girl Leslie told me was coming? I had no idea it would be you. My name is Connor."

***

Connor was fuming after leaving the hotel. The sub-contractor had found yet another way to mess things up. The idiots had hung the abstract art pictures Leslie had purchased upside down. Every single one of them. Oh, not just in one, but in each and every hotel room. As if that wasn't bad enough, traffic was slow. *Should have taken the turnpike.* Instead, he'd made the mistake of taking US 30 on the return from Philly. And since it was Pennsylvania, road construction seemed to be continuous all the way back.

There was so much Connor had to get done on his to-do list today. He needed to place an order for wall coverings, arrange a furniture delivery and Leslie was waiting for a design concept for the Norristown project.

Finally, he turned onto the road where he and his sister lived and wound down his window to breathe in the earthy fragrance of a freshly mowed alfalfa field. Glancing at the clock on the dash, he realized it wasn't quite four. If he hurried, he could still arrange the delivery truck for the Coatesville project tomorrow morning.

Connor jumped out of his pickup, mentally prioritizing his tasks for the next couple of hours. Glancing up, he had to do a double-take as his heart threatened to beat out of his chest. *Is this a mirage?* Seated in a wheelchair was the girl he'd met on the train. *That girl!* The one who'd had her bag taken away. The damsel with the beautiful eyes and long curly hair. *The beauty I dream about all the time. Why would she be here?* He swallowed hard before introducing himself.

The unnamed girl stared at him strangely for a few minutes before nodding. "I'm... I'm Aubrey. Aubrey Stettinger. You're the one they call Connie?"

His face had been warm before, but was now on fire. "I prefer Connor, but you can call me Connie, if you'd like." *Aubrey?* He loved the way her name curled off his lips. *You can call me anything you want.*

Her brown eyes darkened as her lips set into a fine white line. "Why am I getting the impression you knew about this? About me coming here?"

What? "I didn't."

She shook her head. "No. Something about this isn't right. It's, it's like... creepy."

She thinks I'm a creep? "I'm sorry you feel that way."

Aubrey took a deep breath. "And let me guess. You're the one I'm supposed to help. As in, we'll be spending an awful lot of time together, right? Not only working together, but living in the same house. How convenient for you." She certainly didn't look happy.

Guess my first impression of her was wrong. Maybe she wasn't the angel his imagination had concocted. "Is that what Leslie told you?"

She stared at him. "This feels like a setup." She turned the wheelchair from him, rolled further down the porch and pulled out her cell phone.

His sorrow was turning to anger. "If you're not happy about that, fine. You know what? You don't have to help me. I am more than capable of doing what I need without *your* help." Connor shook his head in disappointment. "It was nice to meet you, Ms. Stettinger. I'll make sure to stay out of your way the entire time you're here." He stormed inside.

Leslie was coming down the stairs. "Hey, Connie. Did ya meet our guest?"

His mood was now foul, but he didn't want to take it out on his sister. "Yep."

"Once she gets settled, she can help you."

"I don't think so." He started past her on his way to his room. Leslie grabbed his arm and turned him to face her.

"What's wrong?"

He was still seeing red. "Ms. Stettinger and I have met before. Let's just say... our personalities aren't compatible. I don't need *or* want her help."

"What? Why?"

The front door opened behind them and Aubrey rolled herself into the room. The girl's expression wasn't as severe as before. Connor nodded in her direction. "Ask her. I'm sure she'll fill you in." He stormed up the stairs. "Ask Grey to bring a plate up for me. I'll be working in my room." He cast another glance at the girl. "All night long."

***

I screwed this up. Aubrey called Rachel and told her how she was feeling. Stranded, all alone and set up to be used.

"I think he knew who I was. That's why they brought me here."

"I don't see how. I knew Leslie had a nice place set up for a wheelchair. I'm the one who called her. She helped another friend of mine once before. I've known the Lapps for years and they are nice people."

Aubrey shook her head in disbelief. "So you're telling me this is all a coincidence? That they had no clue who I was?"

"Aubrey, I didn't even tell Leslie your name before you met her. I don't know what to say." Rachel was quiet for a long moment. "Look, I can tell

27

you aren't comfortable about the situation. How about I come pick you up and take you to the rehab hospital?"

Aubrey forced herself to calm down. "Rach, I, uh, guess, maybe I over-reacted."

"Why did you think this was a set-up, that he knew you?"

"The man, he was the one who rescued me on the train, back in April."

She had to pull the phone away when Rachel screamed. "That guy? The one you've been talking about ever since?"

"Um-hmm. Now come on. What's the likelihood I'd end up here, in his home?"

Rachel laughed. "Maybe this was planned."

"Planned? By whom?"

"God."

Aubrey shook her head. "You know I don't believe in God."

The snickering continued. "Just because you don't believe in Him doesn't mean He isn't real." Another long pause. "What do you want me to do? Should I come pick you up, or...?"

Aubrey watched a red-tailed hawk dive bomb at something she couldn't see in a field across the road. The bird flew away, some small animal struggling in its talons. Strange how viciousness and cruelty could abound in a place as seemingly wonderful as this. She shook her head to clear the thought. "No. I fouled up. Let me go in and try to salvage my character. Call you tomorrow."

Aubrey entered the house, catching the conversation between the siblings. After Connor rocketed up the stairs, Leslie turned to her with a look of confusion. "You two know each other?"

"We met, once. A couple of months ago. Some guy took my things on the subway and, and your brother, he, he got them back for me."

Leslie's eyes widened. "Oh my gosh. I don't believe it. You? You're the girl from the train? He hasn't stopped raving about you, even after all this time."

Aubrey's cheeks heated. "Really? I, I, uh, guess that was me."

Leslie eyed her strangely. "Just now Connor said your personalities were incompatible. What did he mean?"

Aubrey couldn't meet the woman's eyes. She fidgeted with her phone. "I, well I, misunderstood."

"Misunderstood what?"

She forced herself to look at Leslie. "I have trust issues." *Especially after what Piotr did, not to mention my youth or when I first got to New York.* "I got it in my head that he knew it was me and... and that was why you brought me here. My fears took over. If you knew about my past, you'd understand."

Aubrey expected that Leslie would explode, but instead the woman knelt next to her and took her hand. "That isn't the case. Neither Connie nor I would do anything to hurt you or make you feel uncomfortable. This house is your home, Aubrey, your safe place. I want you to feel that, in your heart, okay?"

Aubrey's eyes were blurry. *This kindness is so different than...* "I'm sorry. Guess I need to learn to trust and, and also a-a-apologize to your brother."

Leslie smiled. "Don't mind him. He's easy going and if you'd like, I'll smooth it over with him. Want me to do that?"

"No. My mistake, so I need to be responsible. I'll speak with him." Aubrey glanced at the stairs. "Will he really stay up there all night?"

Leslie chuckled. "He does that quite often. His bedroom is also his office." The other woman smiled. "Supper should be ready soon. We're having tacos, Grey's favorite. Do you eat tacos?"

"Yes." *And probably crow, too.* "Need help?"

"It's up to you. Want to set the table?"

"Okay." Before pushing herself into the dining room, Aubrey shot another look upstairs. A sign on the wall caught her eye. It read, *'As for me and my house, we will serve the Lord.'* Aubrey took a deep breath. It was plain to see they were believers. *In action as well as words.* Maybe, just maybe... Aubrey looked at the ceiling. "Okay, I get it. If You're really up there, help me to fit in." It was odd. It felt like a hand patted her shoulder, but when Aubrey turned, there was no one there.

Chapter 3

A ubrey opened her door, a change of clothes in her lap. But before reaching the bathroom, the off-pitch attempt at singing told her Leslie was in the kitchen. The woman had become her friend, but that sure didn't change the fact that Leslie couldn't carry a tune in a bucket. Her host was a great cook and made tasty entrees each morning. *Leslie's so kind to me.* Their friendship was growing rapidly.

Aubrey couldn't say the same about her host's brother. Connor had made good on his word—to leave her alone. For the past week, she'd looked for an opportunity to apologize, but he made sure not to be anywhere near her when it was just the two of them.

The tap of footsteps on the stair treads caught her attention. Connor was completely focused on his phone. *Here's my chance.* She cleared her throat. "Good morning, Connor."

He stopped, two stairs from the bottom. His voice was icy. "Ms. Stettinger. Is there something you need?"

Leslie had told her he would forget about it, but apparently he hadn't. *He's still mad at me.* She swallowed. "There is."

His right eyebrow curved as he surveyed her. "And that would be?"

"Five minutes of your time. We didn't hit it off very well... No. It wasn't us. It was me. I'd like to say I'm sorry. It's just..." She trailed off.

"Just what?" His voice was warmer than seconds before.

"Connor, things... things haven't been going well for me, and, and..." She engaged his eyes and swallowed hard to chase away the warmth in her chest. "It takes a lot for me to trust someone, especially with the day I was having. I couldn't understand why Leslie was so willing to bring me here. And when I saw you, I, I... I'm sorry."

He looked down. "It's not all your fault. I should have been more understanding. Put myself in your shoes instead of..." He started to blush.

What's that about? "Instead of?"

"I made the mistake of judging you."

"You... what?"

"Judged you. I apologize, but I did."

Aubrey shook her head. "I'm confused. What did you judge? Me being in a wheelchair?"

His cheeks turned pink. "No, not that."

"Then can you explain what you mean?"

"That day, on the train, I, uh..."

"Morning. You two want some coffee?" Both of them turned to find Leslie, a smile lighting her face as always. *Why is she always so happy?* It was almost annoying at times.

Connor answered first. "Sure, but I'll get it. I need mine in a to-go mug." He turned to Aubrey. "Aubrey, may I make you a cup? How would you like it?"

His offer caught her by surprise. "Uh, sure. Just black."

When he entered the kitchen, Leslie turned to her. "How'd you sleep?"

Aubrey had to force her eyes off the kitchen door, the one preventing her from seeing Connor. "Pretty well. Those Advil PMs kind of put me out."

Leslie straightened one of the runners on a table. "Do you have a lot of pain?"

"A little, but I'm managing."

Connor returned with the coffee. Hers was in a beautiful cup on a saucer. His was in an official Lapp Interior Design travel mug. "It's a little hot, so be careful." He turned to his sister. "Anything special on the agenda for today?"

"Did you order the carpet for the job in Leola?"

He shook his head. "Not yet. Heading down to Coatesville. Final walk through with the hotel manager. Next, I'm driving to the site in Exeter, then off to Elizabethtown for the Admissions Department project. I'll order the carpet sometime today. What about you?"

"New potential client in Baltimore, downtown. Probably be there all day." She pulled out a couple of sheets of paper from her pocket and gave them to Connor. "Mind going grocery shopping tonight? We need to stock up for the party on Saturday."

Connor's eyes grew wide as he viewed the list. "Good thing I have a truck, huh?"

Aubrey shook her head. "Party?"

Leslie turned and her smile grew even larger. "Yep. The annual Lapp Labor Day party."

Aubrey looked down. "I see."

"Sorry I didn't give you a formal invitation. I assumed you'd be part of it. You're like family to us."

I am? Aubrey turned to Connor. "Really?"

His face broke into a grin. "What she said." He shot her a wink.

Aubrey's mouth was suddenly dry. "O-okay. How can I help?"

Leslie turned her back to Aubrey and faced Connor. She couldn't hear the whispered conversation.

"Of course, where are my manners? Aubrey, would you like to get out of the house? I could use some help shopping." He held the list up for her to see. "This job is bigger than one person can handle alone."

"B-but I'm in a wheelchair. How could I possibly be of use?"

His eyes engaged hers. Those baby blues seemed to touch her, deep inside. *Wow, he's so cute.* Warm feelings, like she'd had that day on the train, promptly increased from an occasional bubbling to a rapid boil. "They have those motorized scooters. I do need to warn you, Leslie complains my shopping skills leave a lot to be desired. And there are things on this list that need a woman's touch." He pointed at the paper. "Matching napkins and tablecloths? I don't even know what that means. Will you please help me?" He slowly stuck out his bottom lip and shot her pitiful puppy dog eyes. "Pretty please?"

She ignored his playfulness. *It would be nice to get out.* "Uh, okay. Since you put it like that. I'd be glad to."

He yanked a pen from his pocket. "Cool. What's your cell number? I'll call about half an hour before I get here. Sound good?" She nodded and recited the number. He gave her his in return. "At least that way you'll know who's calling. Hope you have a nice day. And Aubrey?" He touched her hand, sending tingly feelings up her arm. "If you get bored and want to talk, call me. I'll be there for you, guaranteed. Bye, now." He said farewell to his sister and left.

Leslie turned and motioned with her head. "I've got cinnamon rolls for us. I think this is going to be a glorious day."

Aubrey's head was spinning. *From getting things straightened out with Connor?* "I'm beginning to think so, too."

***

"Looks good to me. Your guys did an exceptional job, plus they finished a week ahead of schedule. Tell your sister I said 'great job'." The man placed the paper on the counter, signed it and handed it to Connor. "When can I expect the invoice?"

Connor neatly stored the completion paperwork away in the tray of his clipboard. "Leslie does the invoicing on a weekly basis, so probably early next week." He shook the man's hand. "Nice working with you, and if you ever have additional projects in the future, give us a call."

Connor climbed into the truck and set the GPS for the office building in Exeter. His hands were shaking as he pulled his cell out of his pocket. She hadn't called. While he breathed a sigh of relief, Connor couldn't help but be a little disappointed Aubrey hadn't contacted him. Had he come on too strong? A voice warned him. *You're playing with fire. If Marci finds out…*

Before he left the parking lot, his cell began ringing. It was Aubrey's number! Of course Marci would order him to ignore it, no matter what he'd told the girl. *But I gave Aubrey my word.* He depressed the button on the steering wheel, preparing to act both surprised, yet professional. "Lapp Interior Design. Connor Lapp speaking."

She hesitated before replying. "Hi. Is this a bad time?"

"No. And this is?" *You know who's calling, idiot.* He was so pathetic.

"Aubrey. Hey, if this isn't a convenient moment, I can call back or better yet, I'll just wait until you pick me up."

Don't let her go. "I'm sorry, Aubrey. Hello. I didn't get your number into my contact list yet, so it came up as unknown." *And now you lied to her?* That was an award winning way to start a relationship. Connor had entered her number as soon as he reached his truck.

"I see. I, uh, was hoping you could tell me where to find the pods for the coffee maker."

She called for coffee? Connor scanned his image in the rearview, noting the look of disappointment on his face. "Cabinet to the left of the sink. Should be a variety of choices there."

"The cup of coffee you made for me this morning was really tasty. What was the flavor?"

She's not in a hurry? Good! "Donut Shop. That's my favorite."

The girl laughed. "Mine, too. How's your day?"

A road construction sign loomed ahead, so he turned on the headlamps and slowed down. "Great." *Especially since you called.* "The office manager signed off on the Coatesville job. Heading up to Reading now."

"Reading? I thought you told Leslie that Exeter was your second stop."

Hmm. She remembered the details of my day? "Exeter's a suburb of Reading." The flag man waved him through.

"Oh, cool. I was worried you added something else to an already busy day." Hmm, now she was concerned about him? "So your morning's been good?" *Didn't she just ask that?*

"Not too bad. How's your day?" *Mine got better as soon as you called.*

"Same old, same old. It gets kind of lonely around here after Leslie leaves and before Grey gets off the bus. So I wanted to thank you for letting me call, but I should probably let you go."

"You can call me anytime. And there's no need to hang up, unless you want to. GPS says I've got forty-five minutes until I get there."

A long hesitation. "Are you sure you don't mind? Like I'm not bothering you?"

He slowed down to pass a bunch of kids walking along the berm. "Not at all."

"C-can I ask you something personal?"

His skin tingled. "Absolutely."

"On the train... why did you help me?"

The memory of that day flashed in front of him. Aubrey was so beautiful, so intriguing. "You looked like you needed a hand. I saw what that guy did to you. It wasn't right."

"And I thank you for that. Not one other person lifted a finger. But I still don't understand. Why did *you* do something?"

Because my heart went out to you. "People are supposed to help each other. The Bible tells us to treat others as we want to be treated."

She huffed into her device. "I'm not a believer, Connor."

That was odd. "Why not?"

"My mom married a preacher when I was just a kid. The things he said in his sermon on Sundays wasn't how he or his sons acted every other day of the week. It was just... Can we change the subject?"

"Of course. No problem, but I want to say something. Don't judge everyone because of one person. Okay?"

There was a slight hesitation. "*Touche.* Can I ask something else?"

"Go ahead."

"That woman who was with you. She didn't like me, did she? I could sense that by how quickly she stood up and hid behind you."

"Her name is Marci, and sometimes, well, she judges people or situations she doesn't understand."

"Is she your girlfriend?"

He swallowed hard. *Right now I wish she wasn't.* "Um-hmm." He could tell she was fishing.

"Alright. Another subject change. You're really close to your sister. Can you tell me about your childhood? I didn't have a close family and always wondered what that would be like."

As Connor drove, he told her all about both of his sisters—diametrical opposites—and their parents. Surprisingly, Aubrey then shared with him about her youth. She never knew her biological father. When Aubrey was eight, her mom married a pastor with four boys, all older than her. Home life had been tough because she'd felt like she was a fifth wheel and was just in the way. Then, her mom got sick with the flu and died when Aubrey was only thirteen. "I'm sorry."

"Yeah, me too." Something about her voice changed. "All this talk is making me tired, so I'm gonna go now. But I am looking forward to shopping with you this afternoon. I'm not used to being cooped up inside for so long. What time do you think you'll get here?"

An idea suddenly surfaced in his brain, bouncing around and almost screaming, 'pick me, pick me'. He couldn't ignore it. "About four. Uh, Aubrey, would you mind if I took you someplace else before we head to Walmart?"

Hesitation. "Maybe. Where?"

"One of my favorite places. I want to share it with you."

"That sounds nice, but you should know I'm not wild about surprises. I'd like to know where we're going... first."

Sounds too much like a date if I say it. "It's, like, really no big deal, but I think you'll like it. Trust me on this?"

A much longer quiet time. "I'm not too good at trusting people." He winced. "But, okay. I'll trust you, maybe just this once."

"Great. See you soon." After she disconnected, he pulled over and made their reservations. *This is gonna be cool.* His entire body tingled.

Chapter 4

A ubrey hoped her face didn't show the excitement welling inside of her. Since that chance encounter on the train almost five months ago, the image of Connor's face had been etched into her mind.

Aubrey shook her head to clear those thoughts when she realized he had retrieved the dratted wheelchair and placed it outside her door. "Want me to help?"

"S-sure." He had lifted her onto the truck seat before leaving Leslie's home. Her legs and back were still tingling from the sensation of his touch. His manly scent had awakened her senses when she wrapped her arms around him even before he lifted her.

Again, he slid one hand beneath her knees and the other around her shoulders. She shivered from the excitement of his touch. As Aubrey again draped her arms around him, a vision came to her. Of Connor holding her tightly while snow blanketed them from heaven. Of their lips softly touching as they melted together... She didn't realize he'd already lowered her to the wheelchair until he tried to pull away. Aubrey still clung tightly.

Connor cleared his throat and whispered, "I don't know if they'll serve us like this."

She quickly released him, her face hot as an iron. "Sorry."

His smile melted her insides. "Don't be. I'd like to welcome you to *Essence of Tuscany Tea Room*. I love the atmosphere. Ever been to a tea room?"

She smoothed her shorts and failed to meet his eyes. "Uh, no. So we're going to drink a cup of tea?"

He laughed. "Better than that. We are having *afternoon* tea."

As they neared the door, a middle-aged lady opened it. Her smile was pleasant. "Connor, so good to see you again." She extended her hand to Aubrey. "I'm the hostess, Jessica Snyder. And you are?"

The essence of sweet fragrances wafting out from inside almost took her breath away. It was Connor who answered. "This is my friend, Aubrey Stettinger."

She swallowed hard. "Hi."

Jessica led them to a higher table that allowed Aubrey's wheelchair to slide under it. Within seconds, a petite blonde with thick hair greeted them, introduced herself as Ashley and took their tea order.

Aubrey felt Connor's eyes on her as she tried to study the menu. It seemed unusually warm, despite the air conditioning. Thoughts of her fantasy still teased her mind. *What is wrong with me? He's got a girlfriend.* "Everything looks good. Do you mind ordering for me?"

Connor's smile was playful. "My pleasure." Within minutes, a tray of small sandwiches and heavenly pastries was delivered by the server. Aubrey's pulse raced from Connor's presence as she picked up a watercress open-faced delight.

"I know you're not a believer, yet, but would you mind if I said grace?"

She quickly dropped the sandwich, remembering that the Lapps did this before every meal. "Sure."

Connor folded his hands. "Father, we thank Thee for this food, the hands that made it and for bringing Aubrey to live with us," he hesitated briefly, "for a while. Lord, please help Aubrey heal, inside and out. Amen."

There was an awkward silence as they ate. *Inside* and *out? How could he know?* She cleared her throat. "I know you're really busy with your job. Thanks for taking time out of your day to bring me here. Your home is wonderful, but..."

Again, the man laughed, sending butterflies to her stomach. "Let me guess, it gets a little boring, huh?"

She studied him. His eyes were kind, so deep and blue, like the sea. "Is it that obvious, or are you a mind reader?"

He finished chewing before replying. "I'm just trying to put myself in your shoes. This must be rough on you, being so far from the city... and even I will admit, Lancaster's not the most exciting place on the planet."

"It sure beats where I was raised in Minnesota. From what I've seen, Lancaster looks nice. But somedays, the smell outside is awful."

"Yes, when the wind is right, you can smell the Stoltzfus dairy farm like it's in the front yard. But don't worry. After a while, you won't even notice it. You'll get used to it."

I doubt that. "When Leslie asked me to move here, I told her I wouldn't take charity. And your sister said I could help you. What can I do for you?"

The blue in his eyes rippled, like sun on running water. "You don't have to do anything, except get better. That's all I want."

She ignored his playfulness. Aubrey's arms tensed. "A deal is a deal. What help do you need?"

The corners of his mouth twitched before breaking into a smile. "If you really want something to keep the boredom at bay, you could be my assistant."

The egg and olive sandwich was tasty, as if coated in sugar. "What would that entail?"

"I don't know. Maybe ordering some supplies. Coordinating jobs with the vendors." His smile grew even larger. "And if you want to get out of the house, you can go with me sometimes when I visit jobsites." His face colored. "As my assistant."

"In my wheelchair?"

"Most of the places I go are handicapped accessible."

She felt her body tense again and her words were sharper than she meant. "I'm not handicapped."

Connor jerked his head and frowned. "Didn't mean to offend you. Let me re-phrase. Most of the places are accessible to people suffering from a temporary lack of mobility."

I over-reacted. "It's okay. It's just so frustrating not being able to walk."

He patted her hand, raising her core temperature a couple of degrees. "I can believe that, but this is only temporary, just a short season in your life."

"Wish this part were over."

He winced. *Oh God, I didn't mean it like it sounded.*

Connor took a sip of tea. "A lesson I've learned, my friend, is that everything happens for a reason."

"Really? What's the reason I got run over by a truck?"

He winked. *Is he flirting?*

"That remains to be seen."

***

Connor parked the motorized buggy next to his Chevy. Aubrey already had the door open and was waiting. He helped her get situated. "Now, for a quick lesson in the finer points of this vehicle."

She shot him a smirk. "I may not have gone to an Ivy League school like Millersville, but I think I can manage."

He pulled the key from the switch. "If you want to use it, you have to suffer through my safety briefing. And as far as the 'Ville," he used the nickname for the university, "it's about as far away from Ivy League as you are from Minnesota." She glared the whole time he was explaining the features of the vehicle.

Aubrey successfully maneuvered her way through the throng of people, abandoned carts and vehicles.

Connor grinned from his elevated position. "You're doing great. See how easy it is when you listen to the safety briefing?"

She nodded her head and mumbled just loud enough for him to hear. "That explains what Leslie meant when she said you were delusional. *Connor has delusions of grandeur.*"

"She said what?"

"It's not important. So how do you want to do this?"

So you want to play, huh? Aubrey was so easy to tease. He'd done it to her quite a bit during their tea. Connor handed her one of the sheets of Leslie's store list and grabbed a cart. "Well, how about if you work on this one and I'll see if I can find everything Leslie wants from the other three papers."

She turned and shot him a confused look. Not for the first time today, he took in those long wavy curls and gorgeous brown eyes. "I don't think that's fair. What if something on my list is out of reach?"

He couldn't contain his chuckle. She'd taken the bait. "Or... we could shop together."

She smiled and it was as if the sun came out of a cloud. "That was your plan the whole time, wasn't it?" She raised her eyebrows. "You're teasing me again, like you've done all afternoon, aren't you?"

He nodded and handed her all the pages and a yellow highlighter. "Why don't you handle the list and I'll do the reaching?"

She was not only gorgeous, but funny as well. Aubrey held his attention by making little remarks about everything from their fellow shoppers to the items on Leslie's list. Though he made sure she didn't see, he couldn't take his eyes off of her. Those brown eyes were so expressive. And her petite hands, so beautiful. Connor also noticed something else. Aubrey kept glancing at him, too. The way her eyes met his made him fuzzy and warm inside.

She was watching him as she turned the corner of the canned goods aisle. The front of her cart clipped a display and several dozen cans of peas hit the floor and rolled in every direction.

Aubrey stopped, eyes wide and put her hand over her mouth. "I didn't, uh, didn't mean to do that."

Connor couldn't help himself. He blurted out, "Clean up in aisle five. Ma'am, if you'd just paid closer attention to the safety briefing..."

"Oh, stop it. Just give me a hand picking up the cans, silly."

Connor continued to laugh while he dropped to his knees and handed her the fugitive metal containers. Aubrey's face was white from embarrassment as she stacked them back on the display.

There was only one left to retrieve. He held the can and offered it to her, but didn't release it when she reached for it.

Her eyes met his. The color in her face slowly returned, then began to turn red. She bit her lip. This wasn't the first time he'd noticed how incredibly beautiful she was, but being this close to her... *I could get lost in your eyes...*

"You're making a scene."

He released his grip on the can and watched her turn away to place it on the pile.

"What the hell are you doing, Connor?" They both turned to the woman standing there. Marci towered above them, hands on her hips, face as red as her hair. Her gaze turned to Aubrey. "And what is *she* doing here?"

Chapter 5

M arci slammed the bowl of macaroni salad on the counter, slopping some of the contents onto the marble surface.

Connor grabbed a paper towel and wiped it up. His girl had been livid in the store, yelling at him to the point of making Aubrey cry. "I still don't understand why *she* has to be here."

Leslie's perpetual smile was gone. "Like Connor told you, I'm the one who invited her."

Marci turned, looking down on Connor's sibling. "Why here? How in the world did you find *her*? And why bring her to this house, where my boyfriend lives?"

Leslie stood her ground. "As I've *already* explained three times, I did it as a favor for an old sorority friend."

The redhead wiped a hand through her short hair. "Yeah, right. I don't like this, not one bit. I want her gone and away from Connor, now." Marci crossed her arms and moved until she was almost touching Leslie.

The shorter girl's words were measured. "This is my home and I'll invite whomever I please. And would you lower your voice? Aubrey is in the next room and I don't want your outburst to offend her." Leslie crossed her arms and stepped even closer to the redhead. "Just so we're perfectly clear on this, Aubrey is my guest and she stays. End of story. "

"Like I really care." Marci whipped around to face Connor. He'd never seen her this angry or her face so scarlet. "Then you'll move out."

He was perplexed. "Why would I do that?"

The woman's eyes went wild. "Did you forget? You were on your knees, like you were proposing to her... and the way you two were gawking at each other. I know what's going on here. You have a decision to make."

"And what decision is that?"

"Either you move out of here, right now, or we're through."

Why was she reacting so badly? "Marci, be reasonable. I was just picking up the cans and..."

"And you held onto the last one. I could see the desire in that harlot's eyes. She's trying to get her claws into you... or does she have them there already?"

Connor shook his head. "You're reading way too much into this."

The redhead clenched her hands in the air as if she were going to strangle someone. "I am not..." She threw her hands down. "I'm going home. If you love me, like you've professed for years, you'll come over. If not, don't ever expect to see me again. You've got one hour to decide your future." Marci stormed out of the kitchen.

Connor and Leslie shared a shocked look. From the next room, they heard Aubrey speak. "I'm sorry,

Marci. It was all my fault, not Connor's. Please don't be..."

Marci's raised voice flowed into the kitchen. "Damn right, it was, you little witch. He's my man. Keep your filthy little fingers off him, you, you, high-foreheaded twit." The slamming of the door shook the entire house.

Leslie eyed her brother. "She's out of control. What are you going to do?"

Connor rubbed his hand across his face. "What choice do I have? I'm following her."

Leslie grabbed his forearms. "Are you an idiot? You know, I've kept my mouth shut while I've watched her bully you for the last three years. She is the most controlling piece of work I've ever seen. And if you marry her, how will that be? If she had her way, I'd never see you again. That woman despises me. She's going to end up tearing our family apart."

"No, no. I won't let that happen." They were both breathing hard. The sound of Aubrey blowing her nose caused him to look at the door. "Leslie, I, uh..."

His sister sighed and then hugged him. "I understand how hard this is for you. Do what you have to do, Connie. You know I'll always be here for you. But if I can make a suggestion, it would be for you to act like a man and stand your ground. Don't allow Marci to rule your life. You're a better person than that, bro." She turned and went in the next room. Connor followed.

Aubrey was wiping her cheeks. Leslie handed her another tissue. "I think it's time for me to leave. I never meant to..."

Enough. Connor walked to Aubrey and touched her hand. "Marci just gets emotional, that's all. Please stay."

Aubrey yanked her hand away. "No. I've caused enough problems... for both of you."

"But Aubrey..."

His sister interrupted. "Can you give us a few minutes?"

Connor needed to soothe the situation. He didn't want Aubrey to feel like this was her fault. "No, I want to..."

Leslie shot him her angry look. "If you're following Marci, do it now. I think Aubrey and I need to have a talk."

Connor surveyed the pair. "Alright. Guess I should go. Have fun at the party." He grabbed his keys, hesitating at the door. He glanced back at Aubrey. Her eyes were shiny as she watched him. Connor turned and walked out.

***

Aubrey wheeled her way down the ramp, a tray of food on her lap. Leslie had convinced her to stay. *For now.*

A white Camaro smoothly slipped into the drive. A tall and handsome man got out. He walked right over to her. "So you must be Aubrey. Connor told me about you, but he certainly didn't do an adequate job." He extended his hand and shook hers. *So warm and soft.* "I'm Joe. Joe Rohrer. Can I give you a hand with that?"

Before she could answer, he whisked the tray from her lap, stood there and smiled. "Okay."

"Hi. Do I know you?"

Aubrey turned to find the source of the voice was Leslie, who was standing behind her. She also had her arms laden with a tray of food, but Aubrey had never seen such a big smile.

The man laughed. "And you must be Leslie, right?"

Leslie's smile somehow increased. "Yes. And you are..."

Aubrey couldn't help but notice his white teeth. "I'm Connor's friend, Joe Rohrer. Your brother talks about you all the time. So much that I feel like I know you. Where is the slacker anyway?"

Leslie's face darkened and her smile disappeared. "He's with Marci. The two had a fight and she threw a temper tantrum." Her face paled. "Sorry. I guess I shouldn't have said that."

Joe laughed. "From what Connor says, that happens all the time. I still don't understand what your brother sees in that woman."

Aubrey couldn't help but notice how Leslie's eyes popped as she took in the man. "That makes two of us. Hey, do you mind giving us some help? With Connor AWOL, we're short-handed."

Joe smiled, but he was looking at Aubrey. "I'd love to."

It took several trips for them to cart all the goodies out to the picnic tables, and Aubrey couldn't help but notice how Joe hung around her. She also picked up on the way Leslie eyed Connor's friend.

Before long, lots of cars arrived, spewing people out onto the lawn. Aubrey tried to find a place away from everyone. She was sitting under the shade of the maple when Joe walked over with a lawn chair. His easygoing smile helped erase the morning's debacle. He plopped down next to her. "So Aubrey, tell me about yourself."

***

Joe was taken by Aubrey and it wasn't just her pretty face. Her voice was sweet. For the first time in years, thoughts of Tara didn't monopolize his mind. Aubrey didn't smile a whole lot, but when she did, it was like a sunny day after a month of rain.

"My dream was always to be an actress. When my mom was still alive, she'd take me for acting lessons in the next town. She believed in me. I finally landed a role on Broadway, just before the accident."

"I'm sorry." Joe couldn't take his eyes off her, though she avoided his gaze. "When did your mother die?"

Aubrey's expression changed and he sensed her pain. "Thirteen years ago. Seemed like my world was ending. The neighbor lady helped out where she could, but..."

Joe offered her the plate of fruit he'd brought over. Aubrey took a slice of watermelon and thanked him.

"How'd she die?"

"She caught the flu. But she refused to go to the doctor right away because money was tight. When my step-father finally broke down and took her, it was too late. The hospital told him Mom had double pneumonia. She died that afternoon." Aubrey brushed her cheeks. "I didn't find out until I got home from school. I never even had the chance to say goodbye."

Poor girl. He touched her hand. "I'm sorry."

"Yeah. Me, too."

She needs uplifting. Ask her, idiot. They sat in silence until he cleared his throat. "Connor told me you get bored, being stuck here. I'm meeting two friends at the Liederkranz in Reading tomorrow for dinner and an evening of entertainment. Would you like to go along with me?"

Aubrey faced him, studying his expression. Her brown eyes clouded and her reaction reflected doubt, as if she was considering whether he was worth it.

"I'm not sure."

Joe could again sense her sadness. *Must be so hard on her, being here alone.* "Okay. If you change your mind, let me know. The place is kind of cool and has a Bavarian feel. I guess I really don't mind going alone."

Aubrey's eyes furrowed, as if she had a bad thought. "It's not that I don't..." She hesitated and looked away. "I, uh, just, uh. I'm having a hard time trusting people."

Joe nodded. "I understand. I've got trust issues myself. Many times people aren't as they seem. Maybe we could do something at another time or, if you don't mind, I could stop by for a visit. Later tomorrow or Monday, on the holiday?"

The girl shivered. "Why would you want me to go with you?"

Because I'm super attracted to you and think you're drop dead gorgeous? He hoped his smile appeared as genuine as he meant it. "I'm just trying to be friendly, that's all."

Again, her eyes took him in, like she was dissecting him. *Or my motives?* Joe was surprised when a tiny smile filled her face. "Sure, why not? I could use a friend."

The sunshine was back. "Great. Isn't this a wonderful day?" *But I've got a feeling tomorrow will be even better.*

Chapter 6

A ubrey studied the eight year old sitting across from her. Grey might be young, but she was smart. Despite the usual giggles, Aubrey sensed something was wrong, evidenced by some of the girl's mannerisms. *I'll wait for the right time to ask her.*

Grey had just popped a six and was contemplating which peg to move on the Trouble board. The little girl's eyes widened as she reached for the blue marker. "One, two, three, four, five, six. Sorry, Abs. That sends you back home." The girl smiled as she returned Aubrey's yellow peg to the slot. "I get to go again."

A knock on the front door interrupted the game. Aubrey glanced up to see her friend Rachel standing on the other side of the screen door. "Rachel!" She addressed Grey. "Excuse me. This is my best friend." Aubrey smiled at the woman. "Come on in."

Rachel's grin was wide. "Boy, it's been a long time since I've been here." She turned to Grey. "And you're Greiston, right?"

Aubrey watched the little girl wrinkle her nose. "How'd ya know?"

Rachel extended her hand to Grey. "Aubrey told me about you. I understand you're the *queen* of board games."

The girl beamed with pride as she shook Rachel's hand. "Yep. Call me Grey. Can I call you Rach?" She pointed at Aubrey. "That's what she calls you."

"Absolutely." Within minutes, Rachel had joined the game and Grey proceeded to give them both a trouncing.

Mimes walked in from the kitchen. "Glory be! If it isn't Rachel Domitar." She hugged Rachel. "I haven't seen you in years. Supper's almost ready. Will you join us? I'm making beef pot pie."

Before Rachel could answer, a loud bang came from the front door. Aubrey could see it was Grey's father. Mimes smiled at him. "Dirk, why don't you come in and sit a spell?"

The man's face was dark. "No, thanks. I'll wait out here. Send the girl out. Soon." He walked away.

Mimes shot Aubrey an angry look and shook her head. "Grey, your father's here."

Aubrey noticed the sad expression on Grey's face. She grabbed her bag, then gave Mimes a hug. She shook Rachel's hand and turned to hug Aubrey, long and tight. The little girl whispered in her ear, "Love you, Abs. Bye." She turned and slowly walked outside, head down.

Mimes shook her head in disgust. "That man..." She swallowed, then turned to Aubrey and Rachel. "I've got to get the pie in the oven. Why don't you girls catch up?" The older woman returned to the kitchen. "About an hour until dinner."

A smile tugged at Rachel's lips. "Love you, Abs? Looks like you're fitting in just fine here."

***

Rachel sat on the porch next to Aubrey. "How's it really going?"

Aubrey sighed. "The Lapps are really nice people. Thanks for suggesting this."

Her friend was fidgeting with her fingers, something Rachel knew meant Aubrey was thinking hard about something. *I'll give her an opening.* "What's on your mind?"

Aubrey studied her. "Connor."

"Hmm. So what's he like?"

Aubrey turned and watched a buggy clip-clop past. "It's funny. He's everything I dreamed he was when I met him on the train. Kind, handsome, sweet. He treats me very nice. I really, really feel like he and I have something special between us. He's the second closest friend I've ever had, besides you. There's just this one tiny thing."

"Which is?"

Aubrey engaged her eyes. "That woman. Marci. Big, mean and she hates me. I told you about the day of the picnic."

"The day Connor left when she ordered him to?"

Aubrey nodded. "Yes. He came home that evening and he and Leslie had a long talk outside. Then he came in and apologized on Marci's behalf, but I really doubt she wanted him to."

Rachel shooed a fly from her face. "Did he tell you what happened?"

"No."

"Are they still together?"

"I don't think so. He hasn't told me any different, but I never see him call her. I overheard him tell Mimes that he thinks Marci is working on a project on the west coast."

"Thinks?"

"Um-hmm. That might explain why he's here every night and not with her."

"Maybe."

Aubrey turned her chair so she was fully facing Rachel. "How could someone as nice as him be attracted to a monster like Marci? And it's not like I can just ask if he dumped her. But I need to know."

Rachel touched her arm. "Ask him, or Leslie."

Aubrey shook her head. "Can't do that. My heart won't let me." Aubrey turned and faced Rachel. It would be impossible to miss the stars in her friend's eyes. "Oh Rach, there's something special happening here. I've never been drawn to anyone like I am to Connor, almost to the point of needing him." She continued to study Rachel's face. "I want to throw my shields away and trust him. But then something inside of me says 'suppose he's just stringing you along, like Piotr did'. Then on the other hand, when I look at him, something shouts out 'he's the one'. And because of that second voice, I'm beginning to wonder if just maybe there really is a God and He really did bring me here for a reason. I just wish Connor would tell me where he stands with her."

Aubrey's brow was furrowed. Rachel's heart went out to her friend. "What does she do?"

"Marci? Some kind of writer. I overheard Connor tell his mother she's working on a screenplay for one of her books."

"She's an author? What kind of books?"

Aubrey sighed. "Romance. Changing the subject. I've got a bigger problem."

The sound of tires in the drive caught their attention. A white Camaro SS convertible parked and the cutest man Rachel had ever seen got out. He retrieved a bouquet of white roses and climbed the steps. He smiled at Rachel, but the look he shared with Aubrey blew Rachel away.

"Good afternoon," he said. "Didn't know you had company." He extended his hand to Rachel. "I'm Joe Rohrer. Pleased to meet you."

At a loss for words, Rachel simply nodded. It was Aubrey who spoke. "Joe, this is my best friend, Rachel Domitar. Rach, this is Joe."

"Hi." His eyes drifted back to Aubrey, but a frown covered his face. "I should have called first." He presented the flowers to Aubrey. "I was hoping we could do dinner and this was my bribe, but I sense now isn't a good time."

Aubrey's face turned pink. "Uh, no it isn't. We were going to have dinner here. I, uh, guess you could join us." Rachel sensed Aubrey's words were hollow.

Joe seemed to pick up on Aubrey's intentions. He shook his head. "I don't want to intrude. Maybe tomorrow night?"

"I don't know. Let me think about it."

Disappointment covered Joe's face. "Okay. Well, I'll go then. Goodnight." He again shook

Rachel's hand. "Nice to have met you." Then he turned and said, "Let me know about tomorrow, Aubrey. I really hope you'll say yes." Head down, he walked away.

They watched him drive off in silence. "Good gracious, Aubrey. It's as plain as the nose on my face."

Aubrey's eyes questioned her. "What's that?"

"He likes, I mean, really, really likes you."

Aubrey drew a deep breath and then sighed. "I know. And that's the issue."

"Him liking you is a problem?"

"Yes. Joe's very nice and I feel a spark with him, too. Now you know my dilemma." Aubrey's eyes trailed the Camaro. "He's Connor's best friend."

Chapter 7

T he three of them were just finishing breakfast. Connor looked adorable in his worn jeans and Millersville golf shirt. He stood and addressed them, but his eyes were on Aubrey. "Anyone want more coffee before I go?"

Leslie answered first. "Nope. I've got a long trip ahead of me and I don't want to have to stop so many times."

He studied Aubrey's face. "How 'bout you, kiddo?" A smile slowly spread across his face, but it was those blue eyes that caught her attention. *Connor's at it again.* Aubrey felt her face heat when he winked.

"Maybe one more cup, if it's not too much trouble."

"For you? No problem at all." He shot her a second wink before leaving the room. *Is he flirting with me, again?*

Leslie cleared her throat. Present on her face was that perpetual smile. "Don't know if you noticed, but I'm here, too."

Intense heat fired up her neck. *I know Leslie suspects something.* Aubrey felt the warmth on her cheeks. She knew she was blushing. "Uh, sorry. I, uh..."

There was merriment in her friend's expression. "I can read you like a book. Want me to tell you what I think is on your mind?"

It was getting hard to breathe. *Please don't. Not ready to admit it, yet.* She lied. "Uh, I'm not really thinking anything."

Leslie laughed. "Oh yes, you are. And I've got a proposition for you. One that will help solve your problem, plus make you feel good."

Oh, no. "Y-you do? What's that?"

"Um-hmm. I can sense it gets lonely after we both leave. I think it's time to spice things up today."

Connor and me? "What are you suggesting?"

Leslie stood and began clearing the breakfast dishes. "I'm meeting with a client in Gettysburg. I'd like you to come along. I was thinking afterwards, maybe you and I could hit the outlets."

Aubrey's pulse began to return to double digits. "Wouldn't I just be in the way, with your client, I mean?"

The other woman shook her head. "Of course not. Connor told me you've helped him get caught up with his work, so maybe you'll be able to assist with mine. Who knows? It might end up being fun. And like I said, afterwards, we'll make a girl's day of it."

Leslie studied her face. This wasn't the first time the woman had offered her friendship. Warmth, though a much different type than Connor made her feel, crept into her chest. "Okay, if I'm not a bother."

Leslie's smile somehow increased. "You are never a bother. It'll be a blast. Just give me a couple of minutes to grab my stuff." Her friend carried the dishes into the kitchen.

Within a few seconds, Connor came through the opening, carrying three travel mugs. He set two down on the table. Connor pointed to one of them. "This one's yours. Black, Donut Shop, just like you prefer."

He always seems to remember every detail. "Who's the other one for?"

He smiled. "For my sister."

"But I thought she said she didn't want more."

His laughter was like a rippling stream flowing down a mountainside. "She doesn't know what she wants sometimes. I made it for her because I can bet she'd end up stopping for coffee within five miles."

Aubrey was curious. "Why did you put mine in a travel mug?"

Connor winked. "Leslie told me she was going to ask you to tag along today. Just trying to make it harder for you to say no." He stretched his back. "But I do hope you said yes. It must be so boring, being stuck here every day. The big G-burg is a cool place." A frown suddenly covered his face. "I'm going to miss talking to you, though."

Aubrey considered this tall man. *I'll miss it, too.* They spoke multiple times every day lately, every time he was traveling. *Actually, I love our calls.* "Maybe I'll check in with you, you know, just to make sure you're awake and stuff."

His eyes danced with levity. He yawned and she could tell it was an act. "Yeah, I am pretty tired. You might have to call real soon, like within the next five minutes."

She ignored the playful comment. "So where are you going today?"

"Checking on the job in Exeter."

"You go there a lot." She tried not to smile. *My turn.* Connor teased her all the time, so this was justified. "If I didn't know better, I'd think you have a girlfriend up there, behind my back. Cheating on me, huh?" His smile left and Aubrey tensed.

He touched her face. "I would never do that." She'd never seen the look that was in his eyes. His words were now but a whisper. A daydream began, with Connor leaning down to kiss her. "Aubrey, I want to tell you..."

"What are you two talking about?" Leslie had returned. Once again, Aubrey's face was on fire. A quick glance at Connor revealed he was also blushing.

He turned away from his sister. "I was just wishing Aubrey a nice day. Heading out now. See you, sis. Talk to you later, Aubrey." The man hightailed it out the door.

Aubrey turned, noting the devious smile on his sister's face. Before Aubrey could think of something to say, Leslie responded. "My brother is such a dork, but deep down inside, he's one of the good guys."

Aubrey nodded, but kept her thoughts inside. *That, he is, but... what was he going to say?*

***

Aubrey repositioned in her wheelchair, Leslie to her left and the man with the wire-rimmed glasses behind the desk. "So, tell me. Why should I choose," he glanced at Leslie's business card, "the Lapp Interior Design Team for this project?"

Aubrey could almost touch Leslie's chipper attitude. "Mr. Douglass, I believe our team can offer you elegant design options that could turn your motel into the most desired lodging in town."

"Uh-huh. Sure you could." He shook his head "How long you been in business, young lady?" It wasn't so much what he said, but the way he said it which bothered Aubrey. As if the man was looking down on Connor's sister. Questioning Leslie's experience, or perhaps it was her character. Aubrey couldn't help but notice Leslie's smile grow larger.

"Almost four years. And in that time, we've completed renovations at over 200 facilities, including twenty-six hotels and motels. May I show you some examples of the projects we've undertaken?" Leslie pulled a large binder from her bag.

Douglass didn't move, but instead stared intensely at Leslie. "What's your customer satisfaction rating? I *assume* you get feedback."

"Yes, sir." Leslie pulled a smaller notebook from her bag and handed it to the man. "We've conducted surveys from each of our clients. Our approval rating is ninety-seven percent completely satisfied and..."

"What about the other three percent?"

"In this package, I have every single review, as well as contact information. You'll note the ones which responded less than completely satisfied are all located in the first tab. If you have questions, please feel free to call them. The Lapp team believes in total transparency."

He took the item and leafed through. Douglass sighed heavily and turned to both women. His eyes fell on Aubrey. "What happened to you?"

Aubrey knew she was blushing. "I got hit by a truck in New York City."

He emitted a demeaning laugh. "Jaywalking?"

Her anger rose. *What a jerk.* She would later wonder what made her say what followed. "No, sir. I started across the street and my eyes fell on a storefront. It was beautiful and I was awestruck. My feet stopped, right there in the street. That's when I got hit. I found out later that it was a Leslie Lapp inspiration." Her entire body heated from the depth of her lie.

He leaned forward, glasses barely hanging on his nose and challenged her. "Really? Which one was that?"

Leslie giggled as she thumbed through the marketing book and opened to a photo. "It was this venue. On Seventh Avenue."

Douglass again eyed them both strangely, but then glanced at the album. He did a double take before grabbing the binder to take a closer look at the picture. "Wow, it is pretty nice." He took off his glasses and dropped them to the desk. "So, if I decide to go with you, tell me how it'll go down."

Leslie turned and shot a wink at Aubrey. "Here's our plan..."

***

Aubrey took her menu from the waitress and glanced at Leslie. The other woman seemed to be struggling not to laugh. Aubrey's brows creased. "What's so funny?"

"You are, you little fibber. A 'Leslie Lapp inspiration'?" The laugh Leslie had been restraining broke free. "Now that was priceless. Are you always this quick-witted?"

Aubrey shook her head. "Sorry, I didn't mean to say that, it was just... I didn't like how he treated you and I wanted to put him in his place." She stopped while the waitress delivered their soft drinks. "I didn't consider that he might ask to see it. Thanks for bailing me out."

Leslie put her hand over her mouth as she giggled. "We did one solitary job in New York City, and that was it." She held her hand up for a high five. Aubrey tapped it. "I'm really glad you came to stay with us, Aubrey."

"Me, too." Aubrey's curiosity got the better of her. "Can I ask a personal question?"

"Of course."

"You're always smiling. Even when Douglass talked down to you. Why?"

Leslie wrinkled her nose. "Do I really smile a lot?"

Aubrey nodded. "Yes, you do. What's your secret?"

Leslie's smile disappeared and she examined her nails. "I was given a second chance at life."

Aubrey shivered at the look on her friend's face. "What happened?"

The perpetual happy smile had been replaced with a sad one. "I was a rebel. Hated everyone and everything. And the one thing I hated more than anything else was... my brother Connor."

Connor? Aubrey pushed back from the table. "You hated your brother? Why?"

Leslie took a sip of her drink, then engaged Aubrey's eyes. "My little brother was perfect. Basketball star, class valedictorian, the apple of my parents' eyes. And I felt like I was nothing in comparison to him, especially to my parents. I was extremely jealous." The older woman wiped her mouth with a napkin before continuing. "We all went on a cruise to celebrate Connor's high school graduation. A couple nights into the trip, I had too much to drink and got into a really bad argument with him." She wiped a hand across her cheek.

"Leslie, if this is too difficult..."

Leslie grabbed Aubrey's hand and squeezed it tightly. "We're friends. No, you're more like family, and besides, you asked. I don't mind sharing what happened with you."

Leslie took a deep breath. "There was a deck party and the two of us were arguing. I don't even remember what we were fighting about. He had me so mad. I started yelling at him and everybody was watching but it didn't affect him. No, not Connor. Instead, he just laughed in my face. I was infuriated and rushed at my brother, intent on hurting him. He jumped aside at the last second and before I knew it, I flew over the railing. I fell overboard."

Leslie's hand was still in Aubrey's grasp. Aubrey squeezed. "What happened next?"

The woman's cheeks were wet. "I never learned to swim. I hit the water hard and started to sink. I knew I was going to die. My entire life flashed before me and Aubrey, I... I was ashamed of the things I'd done and how I treated people. How I'd squandered the gift of life."

The waitress interrupted. "Are you guys ready to order?"

Aubrey turned to face her. "Can you give us a few more minutes?"

The server shrugged her shoulders. "Sure. Flag me down when you're ready."

"Thanks." Aubrey twisted to give her full attention to Leslie. Despite the wetness on her cheeks, a smile filled Leslie's face. "Please go on."

Leslie nodded. "I knew my life was over. My body was sinking, then someone's arms wrapped around me and propelled me to the surface. Suddenly, my head was above the water." Leslie stopped and drew a sip from her drink. "The person I hated most in the world risked his life to rescue me. Connor dived in to save me. My little brother kept my face above the water until the lifeboat arrived." The older woman's eyes caught Aubrey's. "We could have both died that day, but Connor's actions spared me. Gave me a second chance to live. And I changed, right then and there."

Aubrey could only shake her head in disbelief. She was at a loss for words. "Wow."

"Connor's my best friend now. So when you see me smile, it's because I'm thankful for a chance to fix my mistakes and realize every day is a gift. Everything happens for a reason, Aubrey. God taught me several lessons that day... about hatred, and life and especially about love." Leslie's smile had never been as wide as it was now. "And there's a reason God brought you to us, Aubrey. I feel it."

Aubrey was suddenly cold. *Please no. Not a religious lecture.* "And what do you think the reason is?"

Leslie laughed. "Who knows? We'll just have to wait and see." She winked at Aubrey. "My story was pretty heavy. Can we change the subject?"

Please. "Uh, sure."

"I was thinking... I'd like you to help me come up with the design concept for the motel we visited today."

"W-what? Why?"

Leslie's eyes were full of amusement. "I don't know. Guess I thought it would be fun to do it together. What do you think?"

"I'm not sure what I could contribute." Aubrey studied the other woman. *She's trying so hard to be a good friend.* "Why not? I'll try."

Leslie extended her fist, with the small finger offered. "Pinkie shake?"

Like childhood girlfriends would do. "Okay." Aubrey extended her little finger to grip Leslie's.

Leslie giggled. "Partners... and more importantly, friends 'til the end."

Warmth now flooded Aubrey. "Until the end."

Chapter 8

C onnor was driving down Interstate 176 so he could enter the Pennsylvania Turnpike at Morgantown. His next stop would be in Elizabethtown to check on the sub-contractors. He was lonely. Lately when driving, he and Aubrey would talk. Amazingly, they never ran out of things to say. Connor smiled as he thought about their friendship... and how it had grown into... *Love?* The girl was even sweeter than the vision he had concocted of her the day they met. Her face appeared before him.

The ringing of his cell stopped his thoughts. Connor glanced at the display. *Marci?* He allowed the call to go to voicemail, but his mind drifted back to the last time he'd seen Marci. The day of Leslie's party. He had followed his girlfriend to her place, and then walked inside.

Marci stood with her arms crossed. "I was wondering if you were going to come to your senses or not."

He stood in front of her, hands in his pockets. "I'm not very happy with the way you treated my sister, or her guest."

Marci poked her finger into his chest. "Your sister doesn't like me. Never has, never will. And now she brings that little tramp to live in the same house as you? This is unacceptable. Either she goes or you leave."

Connor studied his girlfriend's face. "That's what you stated earlier. Can we discuss this like adults?"

Marci exploded. "What the hell does that mean? You love me. At least that's what you used to say. But let me guess, that's changed since she came along, right?" She moved until their noses were almost touching.

Connor didn't back down. "I fell in love with the woman you used to be."

She all but screamed. "Used to be?"

Connor touched her face. "When we met, you were so kind and sweet and pure. In my eyes, you were the perfect woman."

"And I'm not like that now? Tell me, Connor, when did you fall out of love with me? Let me guess. It was when the little witch arrived, wasn't it?"

Connor noted Marci's chin quiver slightly. For the first time, he saw a chink in the hard exterior. "It was around the time you changed and became a screenwriter."

Her voice was softer. "How did I change?"

"In the way you treat me... and others."

"Again, you're talking about her."

"Not just Aubrey. It's also how you've treated Leslie. And others. Like they're nothing and you are so superior to everyone. I can't and won't take that. Don't act that way to people I care about."

Her face reddened. "So now it's just not the tramp, but your sister, too?"

"Don't call Aubrey a tramp."

Marci nodded, eyes full of fire. "You're breaking up with me, aren't you?"

"That's up to you. Look, I love you, Marci, but we can't go on like this."

His cell sounded again. Marci was calling. Connor swallowed hard before deciding to accept the request.

"Hello?"

"Connor?" There was no anger in her voice, but instead relief. "I was afraid you wouldn't answer. How've you been?"

He slowed to enter the toll plaza. "I've been well. And you?"

He could hear the deep breath on the other end. "I've been miserable. I missed you and have thought long and hard about our discussion. You were right."

"Right about what?"

"About how I've treated people, like Leslie and the other girl... but most importantly, how I've behaved with you."

Connor glanced at the rearview, leaning over and catching the puzzlement in his own reflection. "Okay?"

"Look. I've done some soul searching. I'd really like to try again. Will you give me another chance?"

"Marci, I don't know..."

Marci sniffed. "Once upon a time, you loved me. And I remember you telling me that true love lasts forever. Let me prove to you that we had true love... and still do."

"Marci..."

"Connor Lapp, I love you. I have since the day we met and I've fallen deeper in love with you every day. I don't want to go through life without you. Please, let me show you that I've changed. Let me prove it before you close the cover on our love story, forever. Please?"

Connor brushed his hair out of his eyes. "Marci, I don't know..."

The sound of her sob touched his heart. "I'll take that as a maybe. We'll take it day by day, okay? Please, please, please?"

"Oh, Marci..."

"Look. I'll be back in Lancaster day after tomorrow. Let me drop by, and, and... if I don't treat your sister or the girl like you think I should... I'll leave you alone, forever."

Connor was at a loss for words. "Okay."

Marci let out a sigh. "Thanks, Connor. I won't let you down. I promise." There was a silence. "I love you. Gotta go. Goodbye, sweetheart."

That was the first time she's ever said she loves me. "Bye, Marci. See you then."

Connor disconnected and pulled to the side of the road. His limbs were shaking. Marci's spell was broken. *What did I just do?*

***

Aubrey wheeled her chair outside, while Leslie stood in line to pay the bill. Aubrey had used the excuse of going to the restroom, but that wasn't the truth. She dug her phone from her bag, unlocked the screen and selected Connor's number. Despite having an extremely fun day with Leslie, Aubrey missed

Connor, terribly. Just the thought of him made her warm all over. Their daily talks had increased to fill not only his driving times, but often continued late into the night. One night, their conversation was still going strong when the sun came up the next morning. And one thing had become evident. *The attraction between us is not only strong, it's mutual.*

Aubrey was afraid to consider the 'L' word, yet, but the thought teased her constantly. She quickly called, breathlessly waiting for him to pick up.

"Hi, Aubrey." As soon as he answered, she could tell something wasn't right.

"Hey. Are you okay? You don't sound like your normal self."

"Yeah, it's just, well... nothing important."

Deep inside, a nagging feeling took root. "It must be something. I can hear it in the tone of your voice."

He exhaled sharply. "I'm just irritated, that's all."

She glanced at her watch. There'd been a host of issues at one of the jobsites that required his frequent supervision. "Problems in Exeter? Is that where you're at?"

Hesitation. "I'm heading to E-town. Actually, things aren't going bad in Exeter. It's... uh... another development."

Whatever had him unnerved started a chill that climbed her spine. "Would you like to talk about it?"

"I... I can't."

What? Over the last couple of weeks, they'd spoken about everything. Except one subject, *Marci.*

Aubrey's mouth grew dry. "Come on. We're friends. I thought you and I could share everything. Or has that changed?"

"No, no. But Aubrey, I, uh... this is hard."

Why would he shut me out? She took a deep breath. "I see. Well, I'll let you go then."

His response was immediate. "No, please don't hang up. It's not that I don't want to talk to you, but I'm afraid... Aubrey, I don't want my issues to *ever* come between us. Can we talk about some other topic? How's your day been?"

He'd changed the subject to cover the issue. *To protect me or hide something from me?* Over the next two minutes, she gave an abbreviated version of her day. But whatever was going on with him... she knew he needed her. "Connor, come on. We're close. Whatever's bothering you, I want to help. You do know you can trust me, right?"

He sighed. "Absolutely. You're special, Abs. Do you know that? Never known anyone like you." Within the last week he'd started calling her 'Abs'. "Can't hide anything from you, can I?"

No, I know you too well. A warmth replaced the chill inside her chest. "Afraid not. We're too close. Come on. Spill the beans."

"Okay. Here goes." He hesitated. "I did something tremendously stupid."

I doubt that. "Such as?"

"I'll tell you, but first, promise me you won't be mad at me, please?"

"Okay, Connor. You're scaring me."

He blurted out his response. "Marci called."

I knew it! Even though Aubrey was certain they'd broken up, she didn't want him to know she knew. "How was that a problem? She's your girlfriend, right?" *Tell me different, please?*

His voice was soft. "She was, but the day of the picnic, she and I had a fight. I told her I couldn't... let's just say I gave her an ultimatum and she... Marci walked away from me."

Yes! Though excited, Aubrey forced her voice to be calm to support the next untruth. "I, uh, didn't know that. Then why did she call?"

Aubrey could hear his turn signal. "She wants me to give her another chance."

What? No, no. She blurted out, "Are you going to do it?"

"I, uh, I don't know."

His breath was ragged. Aubrey's hands were shaking. *Just when I was beginning to trust you.* "Why would you?"

"Abs..."

Time for the moment of truth. "Do you still love her?"

A long pause. "I loved and still do love the girl... the girl she used to be. I-I'm just not sure... about anything right now."

"Does Marci love you?"

"Today was the first time she ever told me she did."

Aubrey was seeing red. That woman couldn't possibly love him, not with the way she'd acted that day. *This needs to be said.* "Connor, forgive me for sticking my nose where it doesn't belong. I may not be a believer, but I remember my step-father's sermons about love. Probably the only thing he ever said that made sense. I think it was from First Corinthians. He preached that love is patient. Love is kind..."

"Aubrey..."

She ignored the interruption. "Love is never boastful or wanting its own way. I can't remember the rest, but after seeing the way Marci treated you? Was that really love? I highly doubt it. Instead, I think this is her way of trying to exercise control over you."

"You're not helping."

Connor! "Open your eyes. Did she really mean she loved you, or is it a ploy to get you back under her claws?"

"I-I'm not sure."

Aubrey's hopes were rapidly fading. "I see. You *do* love her, don't you?"

"I really don't know."

All the warmth was gone. "Okay. Hey, gotta go now. See you later."

"Abs, wait..."

Aubrey disconnected and dropped her phone on her lap. *He is just like Piotr.*

"Hey, are you alright?"

Aubrey turned to see Leslie standing next to her. Aubrey swallowed hard, choked back a sob and nodded.

Leslie lightly touched her arm. "I know you better than that. What's wrong? Who were you talking to?"

Aubrey brushed a hand across her cheeks. "Connor."

Leslie's face paled. "Is he okay? What happened?"

Her cell rang again. Connor was calling. Aubrey declined the call and began to roll her wheelchair away. "Marci. That's what happened."

Chapter 9

Leslie peeked between the gap of the kitchen door and the frame. She wanted to eavesdrop on the conversation between Aubrey and her brother, but there was a problem with that. A big one. They weren't talking. From Leslie's viewpoint, she could see Connor was pretending to read, but he couldn't keep his eyes off the girl in the wheelchair. Aubrey, on the other hand, was doing a very convincing job of ignoring him while she worked on her laptop. When Leslie had walked past earlier, she'd seen Aubrey was searching for ideas for the Gettysburg project.

Leslie whispered out loud. "Come on, Connor. Tell Aubrey you made a mistake and that you're going to end it with Marci. Let Aubrey know how you feel about her." How could her brother be so intelligent, yet so stupid? Both Leslie and Mimes could tell Aubrey was *the* one for him. That she loved him, whether she'd said it out loud or not. Connor was a smart man. Surely he knew, didn't he?

The oven timer sounded. Leslie silenced it and grabbed the stack of dishes so she could set the table. But before Leslie could leave the kitchen, a knock sounded on the front door. Leslie walked into the dining area. Aubrey closed the lid on the laptop and turned to her.

"Let me put this away and I'll be right back to help." The curly-haired girl directed her wheelchair away from the table.

Leslie glanced at her brother. He frowned, then opened the door and Marci stepped in. *Oh look. It's the red-headed witch of the east.*

Connor paused for a moment, as if he would change his mind. "Hi, Marci. May I take your coat?"

"That would be kind. I missed you so much, Connor." Leslie's stomach turned as she witnessed Marci kiss her brother's cheek. Like Judas had kissed Jesus when he betrayed the Lord in the garden.

You mean you missed running Connor's life. Why in the world had he taken her back? After the humiliating way she'd acted the day of the party. When had her brother evolved into an idiot?

Marci approached and lightly hugged Leslie. Leslie's body began tingling in a bad way, as if she'd just been exposed to the plague. "Hi, Les."

"I hate being called that. As I've told you before, my name's Leslie. I prefer to be called that in the future, thank you."

She expected the red-haired girl to say something nasty, but instead Marci took Leslie's hands and smiled. "I'm sorry. I promise not to make that mistake again. You look really nice tonight."

I see right through your act. "Thanks."

Marci smiled and then rotated slightly. Her expression appeared genuine as she spoke. "Good evening, Aubrey."

Leslie noted Aubrey's eyes were blank. "Hi."

Marci walked around the table and sat so she and Aubrey were facing eye to eye. "I owe you an apology for the way I treated you."

"Apology accepted." Aubrey quickly maneuvered her chair away from the other woman and picked up the dishes from where Leslie had placed them. She started to set the table.

Marci swiveled so she was facing Aubrey. "No. I really mean it. I acted like a fool that day."

Aubrey organized the silverware around a plate. She appeared to be concentrating on her task. The words she spoke were measured. "Your act might fool Connor, but I see right through it." From the corner of her eye, Leslie caught Connor's double take. Aubrey moved on to the next place setting. "Don't pretend you like me, because you don't. And I really don't care. In a couple of weeks, my casts will come off and I'll return to New York, where I belong. Out of your way. So quit pretending and save your breath. You and I both know you don't mean it."

"No, you're mistaken. I've changed, Aubrey. I want to apologize so we can be friends."

Aubrey gathered the last place setting and wheeled herself over to Leslie. She handed a single plate and some silverware back to Leslie before spinning the chair to face Marci. "You and I will never be friends. We had one thing in common and now that's gone. Don't waste one more second of your precious time on me."

Marci stood in front of Aubrey. She looked as if she would cry. "I know you're angry, but please. Can I have a second chance?"

Aubrey ignored Marci and focused her attention on Leslie. "The food smells scrumptious, but I'm not eating dinner here."

What? "O-okay. Would you rather eat in the kitchen or your room?"

Aubrey flashed her a smile, but Leslie could see the sadness in it. "No. I'm going out. I have a date. Thanks anyway."

Connor walked over and stood next to Leslie. "A date? With who?"

For half a second, Leslie caught a glimpse of something in Aubrey's eye. *Sadness? Anger?* No, disappointment. The woman replied, but her gaze remained on Leslie. "With Joe Rohrer."

***

Joe shifted the lever into park. His entire body tingled in anticipation as he opened the car door. *Can't believe she asked me to take her on a date.* He'd almost given up hope that Aubrey would ever go out with him again.

It had been a long time since he'd felt this happy. A full moon hung in the sky with dark purple and silver tinged clouds softly framing the lunar surface. He strode up the ramp, the thought of being with her filling his mind.

Aubrey was sitting outside, a light wrap across her shoulders to ward off the early autumn chill. Tonight, her hair was pulled back, a clip holding the beautiful curly locks away from her face. She pivoted the chair slightly and he could see her face in the porch light.

"Good evening, Joe. And thanks for your spontaneity." Aubrey was smiling. Her beauty almost took his breath away.

"Your invitation caught me by surprise." Even in the dim light, those beautiful brown eyes gleamed. "You look exceptionally lovely tonight."

She laughed. "Flattery will get you everywhere."

Gentlemen Prefer Blondes? Had she known how much he loved that movie? "In that case, we won't have any problems." Her eyes were laughing. "And just so you know, I prefer brunettes, not blondes."

Aubrey raised her eyebrows and nodded in the direction of his car. "Shall we?"

"Sure. Mind if I stick my head in and say hello to Connor?"

Her face clouded. "It's up to you, but I need to warn you. Marci's inside."

Marci? I thought Connor said they were through. "That's a surprise. Why's she here?"

"None of my business and I don't really care. After the way she treated me the day of the party, I don't want to be within ten miles of her." Aubrey's smile grew. "Tonight, I wanted to be with someone kind. Somebody I like. And that, dear friend, would be you."

Is this a joke? Joe had been attracted to this young lady since he met her at the Labor Day party. But she'd been quite standoffish, even when he took her to the Liederkranz. And now? Why the change? *I don't care why, I'm just glad.* Her words brought him back to the present.

"Are you stepping inside or shall we go?"

He cast a glance at the door, then turned to her. "I'll let you in on a secret, I don't like her either. I'd much rather spend time with you, *dear friend.* Let's leave."

Her laughter was like spring rain on a tin roof.

Joe pushed the chair down the ramp and helped her into the Camaro. Sitting behind the wheel, he glanced in her direction. Once again, those brown eyes were sparkling. "So... where do you want to go?"

"Well, we have a couple of options. Are you in the mood for steak or seafood or... might I suggest, perhaps a hibachi restaurant?"

His mouth was watering, but was it the thought of the food or the plumpness of her lips? "I like the hibachi grill idea."

"Well, that settles it. I did some research. It looks like there's one with pretty high ratings near Park City. Ever been there?"

"Yep. I like the atmosphere... and the shrimp."

Aubrey laughed. "Are you sure it's not the sake?"

Joe shot her a wink. "You caught me. Of course, it's really the sake."

"Then let's go."

"Whatever the lady wants." Joe turned on the headlamps and backed the car into the road. The high beams illuminated a figure standing on the front porch. A hand was raised in farewell and Joe caught the sad expression. The path of light swept away from the person, leaving Leslie alone in the gloom of the night.

***

Connor's eyes followed Aubrey as she rolled out of the door.

"Connor, I'm sorry." Marci stood watching him. "I did what I promised, I tried to be nice to her. She just doesn't seem to like me."

"Too bad you weren't this kind in the past." Leslie's arms were crossed as she faced Marci.

Connor shuddered, expecting Marci to blow up.

Marci stepped closer to Leslie. "I can't go back in time and change what happened. I doubt you'll believe me, Leslie, but I've changed. Connor's ultimatum made me assess who I was and what I'd become. I realized I'd turned into something I never intended to be, a nasty person. I did some soul-searching and knew I had to change."

Leslie shook her head and walked to Connor. She touched his hand. "Doesn't this sound familiar at all, Connor? She's bamboozling you and like a fool, you're falling for it, again. This is exactly what Marci intended to do by coming over here tonight. A perfectly crafted plot to drive a wedge between you and Aubrey. Can't you see what's going on? You're letting your future go because you're holding onto a sliver of the past. You know this in your heart as well as I do."

Connor could easily read Leslie's mind. She thought Marci had just driven Aubrey away. *Permanently?*

Leslie took a deep breath and walked out to the porch, slamming the door behind her.

He shook his head. *Leslie's right. What am I doing?* He turned to Marci. Her eyes were moist.

"Connor, I know what's important now. I love you. Don't listen to your sister. I've never been more honest with you than I am right now. It's not my books or the screenplay that really matters. It's you. For three years, you've expressed your love and I was silent, when I should have told you how I really felt. I was a fool."

How could I be so stupid? "No, you weren't. I'm a buffoon. An idiot for believing that you and I could turn this around. Know what? I do *not* love you anymore. We're done."

Marci pivoted away from him, her shoulders heaving as she cried.

It felt as if his heart was being torn out of his chest. Not because of Marci, but instead from considering how Aubrey must feel. Quickly he ran out onto the porch. Leslie was standing in the night, head pointed down the road. "Am I too late?"

His feet were glued to the porch floor as he waited for Leslie's response. His sister slowly confronted him. The perpetual smile on her face was gone, now replaced with sadness. The light from the interior briefly lit the deck. Marci walked past both of them without a word, except for her sobs. Leslie was still searching Connor's face as headlamps lit the porch again. The sound of Marci's Beamer driving off faded.

"She won, Connor. Marci achieved her objective. She drove Aubrey away from you and into the arms of another man." Her face screwed up as she shook her head. "How could you be so dumb and naive? I hope you're proud of yourself."

His mouth was dry. "I was trying to be honorable, I guess."

Leslie shoved him, her voice raising in volume. "And was it worth it? You must be blind or completely stupid." He didn't know what to say. "You're an idiot. I'd never seen you as happy as you've been since that young lady moved in. Couldn't you see how much Aubrey loved you? And what did you do? You stuck a knife in her back by letting Marci drive her away."

"Loved? Do you really think it's too late?"

Leslie studied him for a long while. "I hope not, but I guess only time will tell."

Chapter 10

T he house was quiet and had been for the past hour. Aubrey was pretty sure both Leslie and Connor were gone for the day. She slowly opened the door and discovered she was right. Aubrey was all alone.

The scent of pumpkin spice subtly filled the room. Leslie had left a candle warmer turned on. Despite waiting until they were gone, she missed them both. Rolling into the kitchen, she found a pair of notes waiting for her. The light violet one on the refrigerator door had a smiley face. Aubrey recognized the writing as Leslie's.

Hey sleepy head,

Good morning. There's a plate with a pepperoni, black olive and feta cheese omelet hiding in here (plus a little surprise). Find it, and it's yours. I'll be back mid-afternoon and was thinking about taking Grey to Flinchbaugh's Orchard to get Halloween decorations. Want to join us? It'll be fun. Text me. Have a great day, Leslie

The plate Leslie had hidden was sitting behind the milk carton. A Reese's pumpkin candy lay on top of the aluminum foil. Aubrey ate the peanut butter filled delight while she waited for the microwave to heat her food. Connor's message waited over by the coffee maker and beckoned her to read it. Aubrey intentionally ignored the paper, brewing a cup before transporting her meal to the dining room table.

She had just taken her first bite when a sharp knock sounded on the front door. She rolled over and swung the door open. A lady held a beautiful flower basket. She seemed nervous as her gaze took in the interior. "G-good morning. This delivery's for an Aubrey Stettinger. Is that you?"

Aubrey nodded. "Oh, they're beautiful. Thanks."

The delivery girl hesitated. "No problem. I know it's none of my business, but didn't Connor Lapp used to live here?"

"He still does. Why do you ask?"

The woman's face reddened. "Oh, sorry. I was just curious. He and I dated a few years ago, that's all. He's a wonderful man... and you're, you're very lucky." Something about the porch decking must have been very interesting because the lady's attention seemed to be focused on it. "When you see Connor, tell him Christine Berryman said hello." When she looked up, her expression was wistful, her eyes watery. "Congratulations, by the way." She scurried off to her delivery van.

Congratulations? Christine must have thought she and Connor were married, or at least together. *What would that be like?* Aubrey closed the door and a vision of Connor's face filled her mind. *Damn you, Connor. Couldn't you tell I was falling in love with you?* She navigated to the table. *Why'd you have to be like Piotr?*

The tone on Aubrey's cell resonated from her bedroom where she'd left it so she would have an excuse why she wouldn't be talking to Connor today. Still, she hurried back to check the caller ID. Surprisingly, it wasn't Connor. She took a deep breath before accepting it.

"Morning, Aubrey."

"Well, if it isn't Joe Rohrer, sake connoisseur supreme. How are you this morning?"

He laughed. "Much better, *now.*"

Now? "Was something wrong?"

"No. It's simply that my day improved a hundred fold just by hearing your voice. I wanted to thank you for calling me last night. And for the wonderful time we had."

"I had a nice evening, too."

It was easy to hear the teasing in his voice. "So, based on our mutual previous pleasant experience, might you be available tomorrow to continue enjoying each other's company? A little birdie told me the Strasburg Railroad has a cheese and wine train gliding on the rails to Paradise Saturday afternoon. I was hoping we could start there and maybe gravitate to dinner afterwards." Joe's voice sobered. "All joking aside, would you like to go with me?"

Last night had been nice. "Sure, why not? And thank you for the flowers."

"You're welcome. I remembered you told me white was your favorite color, so I hope you like the roses. I've got to head into the office. May I phone you tonight?"

Roses? They must have messed up the order.

"I'd like that. Thanks for calling. Have a great day, Joe."

"Talking to you made it a perfect day. Bye, Aubrey."

She had no sooner placed the cell back on the bedside table when a loud rap again sounded on the door. Aubrey retraced her path and opened it. This time, it was a man standing outside, holding a large bouquet of white roses. His smile was pleasant. "Delivery for Stettinger."

"That's me." He placed the arrangement in her arms and departed.

Aubrey found the card.

Aubrey, Thank you for last evening. These flowers are lovely, but could never compare to how beautiful you are to me. Thanks again, Joe.

If these were from the doctor, who sent the other arrangement? She lifted the basket and searched, but couldn't find a card.

Puzzled, Aubrey reached for the waste wrapping paper. That's when she found it. Her mouth went dry as she read, then re-read the handwritten message.

Nicely played, Aubrey. You won this battle, but the war's just beginning. I'd suggest you quit while you're ahead, but my gut tells me you're too proud to roll away and leave. So, game's on. Everyone has a skeleton in their closet. Don't worry, I'll find yours and expose it for the world to see. Good luck, you little witch. You'll need it because I never lose.

***

Aubrey maneuvered out of Leslie's SUV. No matter how many times she'd climbed in and out of vehicles, it was still awkward. Grey pushed Aubrey's chair away from the Suburban and closed the door. The girl's expression seemed melancholy. During the ride to the orchard in York County, Grey had barely said two words.

Leslie came bouncing around the corner. "Do you remember this place, Grey? Mimes and I brought you here last year."

The little lady's head was down. "I think so. We went on a wagon ride or something."

"Not just the wagon ride, we also did the corn maze and then the apple slingshot. And you picked such beautiful pumpkins to decorate the house, remember? Maybe you can pick some out for us today. Would you like that?"

Aubrey was confused. "Apple sling?"

Leslie was giggling. "Um-hmm. You can buy a bucket of apples and there's this sling shot device. You aim at targets. We had so much fun. Of course, we'll be making a little wager, won't we, Grey?"

"Sure."

Leslie's smile vanished. "Are you okay, honey?"

Grey dug at a bare spot in the grass with her toe. "Yeah."

Leslie touched her cheek. "You sure?"

"Uh-huh."

"Okay. You know if something's bothering you, Aunt Leslie is always here for you." Grey didn't answer, but feebly nodded her head. Leslie shot Aubrey a concerned look. "Why don't you two look around and I'll go buy us tickets for the events." Grey wasn't looking when Leslie signaled Aubrey to see if she could find out what was going on. The pair watched Leslie head to the orchard store.

Aubrey grasped the wheels. "Want to check out the pumpkins?" But Grey didn't move. Aubrey's eyes fell on the girl's face. Little tears were tracking from her eyes. "What's wrong?"

"I was a bad girl. Mommy and Daddy hate me."

"What? No, they don't. Why do you think that?"

Grey's bottom lip was sticking out as she sobbed. "Mommy has a boyfriend. I woke up and he was in the kitchen making breakfast. Mommy was still sleeping."

Oh no, please no. Aubrey reached for Grey's hands. "Did he touch you or say anything mean to you? You can tell me."

"No. He just said hi and took breakfast back to Mommy's room. I told Daddy about him when I went to his house that night. Daddy was mad and called Mommy." Grey reached for Aubrey's hand. "They had a big fight. It was so loud. I went to my room, climbed into bed and covered my head."

"What happened next?"

"Daddy was so mad at me. He threw the door open, screamed at me and didn't even tuck me in. He told me I was a very bad girl."

"Oh sweetheart, you didn't do anything wrong and you certainly aren't bad."

"Mommy said I was a tattletale. She told me not to tell Daddy none of her business no more. Mommy said I was horrible and she was sorry she ever had me."

Grey wrapped her arms around Aubrey and clung tightly.

"If they send me away, can I stay with you? Will you be my new mommy?"

Aubrey's vision blurred. Her mind traveled back in time. To when she was a little girl, before her mom married the preacher. And how sometimes Aubrey would find strange men in their apartment when she woke in the morning. And the yelling and screaming that always seemed to follow. Her heart went out to Grey. "Of course I would, but that won't be necessary. Your mommy and daddy love you and would never make you leave."

"Are you sure?"

"Yes. Sometimes adults get mad at each other and have fights. It's normal." *But it's not ever acceptable to take it out on your child.*

"Really? I never heard mommy and daddy do that before." Grey walked slowly beside Aubrey. "Do you and Aunt Leslie fight?"

"No. We're good friends."

"How about you and Uncle Connie?"

Aubrey stopped, contemplating not only what Grey had said, but also the deeper meaning. Was

Grey comparing them to her own parents, as a couple? Connor's face again flashed before her.

"Do you?"

Aubrey shook her head to chase away his image. "Do I what?"

"You and Uncle Connie. You know, fight?"

"We, uh, disagree sometimes, but no. We don't yell or scream about things. We talk our problems out." *Really?*

Grey hugged her tightly. "I want to stay with you. You're my best friend ever. Love you so much, Abs."

Her mind returned to her childhood. The loneliness. The sadness. She drew Grey deeper into her arms. The little girl sniffled. "I love you, too. Don't cry, sweetie. It will be fine. I'll always be here for you."

***

Connor checked his phone, again, before throwing it down. Nothing, nada, zilch. *Did I ever screw up this time?* Last night had been all for show. As if Marci had scripted it. Oh, he'd seen the pleasure in his ex's eyes when Aubrey left. It had all been an act. *And I played my part, as the fool supreme.* He'd hurt Aubrey... No, worse yet, he'd allowed Marci to hurt her while he stood there and watched without lifting a finger to stop it. No wonder she hadn't called or texted.

The shrillness of his ring tone stopped the pity party. He quickly retrieved the device from where he'd tossed it on the other bed. *Please be Aubrey.* But it wasn't. It was Leslie.

"Where in God's name are you?"

"I decided to stay overnight."

"In Baltimore? Why?"

"The project's not going well. The property manager and the crew supervisor had a tiff. Seems they have a bad history and can't get along. Felt like I was playing referee all day."

Leslie was quiet momentarily. "Is that the only reason?"

No. I haven't figured out how to fix this yet. "Yes."

"I think you're lying, but I don't have time to deal with your issues right now. We have a serious problem."

He shook the cobwebs out of his head. "What's going on?"

"Lisa and Dirk apparently had a major blow up. And poor little Grey's stuck right in the middle."

For the first time all day, Connor's issues no longer mattered. "What happened?"

Leslie told him what Grey had confided to Aubrey. "Then, when he picked up Grey, he treated her like she was nothing. Screamed to get her butt in the car. Treated that little girl like she was a bother to him." Leslie stopped and sniffed. "Connie, we can't let him dishonor our niece like this. Going through the divorce was bad enough." Leslie's voice rose an octave. "Poor Grey. Connor, I need your help. I don't know what to do."

"Maybe we should talk to Lisa."

"I called her already. It was not a pleasant conversation."

Connor slicked back his hair. Ever distant, his eldest sister Lisa had always been the wild one, preferring to be a lone wolf rather than part of the family. "What did she say?"

"I believe she's started drinking again, or worse. Told me she finally found the man of her dreams and everything would have been great if Grey hadn't opened her big mouth and blabbed it to Dirk."

"Poor little Grey."

Leslie's voice trembled higher. Even through the phone, he could feel his sister's sadness. "And I really upset her when I reminded her she had a responsibility... that she has a daughter."

Connor shook his head. "You know that's her hot button."

"I didn't mean to, it just came out."

"How'd she react?"

"Blew her top like Mount Saint Helens. She screamed at me and told me if I thought being a parent was so easy, then I should just adopt Grey." Leslie stopped and sobbed. "What she said next tore my heart out."

Connor hesitated. "I'm afraid to ask. What'd she say?"

"Lisa told me she and Dirk never wanted children. Said Grey was a mistake both of them wished they'd never made. That neither one of them wants the responsibility of her living with them and... that they're seriously considering giving her up for adoption."

Connor's entire body trembled in anger. "We can't let them do that. Maybe it was just the alcohol talking. How's Grey?"

"Aubrey and I took her over to Flinchbaugh's Orchard in York County to try and cheer her up. The girl's super depressed. Know what Grey asked Aubrey?"

The image of Aubrey's pretty face, framed in that long curly hair surfaced in his mind. He forced it out. "What did she ask?"

"Grey asked Aubrey if she would be her new mommy, if her parents sent her away."

"Good Lord."

"I know you're staying there because of what happened last night with Marci. But I want you here, tomorrow. Grey needs you."

"I'll be there."

"And not just Grey. We all need you."

He nodded. "I promise I'll be there for my girls."

"You better be. Good night."

Connor sat there after they disconnected, staring at the wall. *Why were Dirk and Lisa so stupid?* Couldn't they see what they were doing to their daughter? And the answer to the problem was so apparent. Why couldn't people just do the right thing?

"Like you do?" The voice seemed to come from nowhere, yet everywhere. It was so loud that he stood and looked around for the source. *People doing the right thing? You mean like you did last night?*

Chapter 11

A ubrey glanced at the clock. Grey would be getting off school in an hour. Aubrey redirected her attention back to the laptop. She had just finished the outline of her design concept for the Gettysburg job. Starting at the top of her summary, she ran through her ideas. Though she tried, Aubrey couldn't really concentrate.

In frustration, she sighed and closed the computer. *Life is cruel.* What was wrong with Lisa and Dirk? So selfish. Dumping their issues on poor little Grey like that could cause permanent emotional damage. The girl needed a stable, loving home.

Lightning flashed outside. A perfect contrast to the steady rhythm of the rain. Mother Nature had been trying to lull her to sleep all day with a soundtrack of raindrops, wind and the low rumble of far off thunder.

Aubrey brushed the hair back from her face. A vision filled her mind when she closed her eyes. Of a baby in her arms. So small and defenseless. Her daughter, so sweet, so perfect. She leaned down to kiss the child. *I'll always love and protect you.* A voice called her name. She turned to the source and saw him. Connor. He smiled and reached for her, lips inviting as he drew her close.

"Aubrey?"

The touch of fingers on her shoulder abruptly interrupted the fantasy. Connor *was* standing before her. "Sorry. Guess I must have dozed off."

"Didn't mean to disturb you."

"No worries." She suddenly wanted him to hold her. But was it because of the daydream or the sadness of Grey's plight?

Connor looked uncomfortable. He sat across from her. "Leslie and I spoke last night. She brought me up to speed with what's going on with Grey."

Aubrey exhaled sharply through her nose. "Her parents are idiots for treating her like that. You should have seen the grief on that child's face."

"That was what Leslie said. I'm going to pick her up from school today."

Aubrey nodded. "I think that's a good idea."

He studied her eyes. "A better one would be for you to come, too. The two of you have a special bond and I know she'd appreciate you being there."

Aubrey quickly glanced outside at the deluge. "It's raining cats and dogs. I'll get drenched." She couldn't meet his eyes. *I'm a little scared to be with you right now. Scared I'm not strong enough.* "Besides, you're mistaken. I mean Grey doesn't really need me... to come along."

His bright blue eyes seemed to glow. "Yes, she does. I don't believe you understand how important you've become to my niece..." She could feel the warmth beckoning her to wrap herself in him. Aubrey's vulnerability grew as his eyes soaked her in. "And to everyone else in this household."

A few days ago, I'd have given my arm to hear that. She turned her head to keep from falling under his spell. "Connor, I appreciate you saying that, but let's face the facts. I'm just an invalid your sister took in. In a few weeks I'll be taking the train back to New York."

She chanced a glance and couldn't look away. His eyes grew soft and she was drawn to him like a moth seeks a flame. "No, that's not entirely true. Leslie did take you in, but you're wrong. Please don't think you're just someone staying here. You've become a friend, no... more than that. You're part of the family now. This, this is where you belong."

There was a time when your words might have been true. "It's soon time to go home."

He pushed back his chair and stood. The blue in his eyes seemed to flare up. "And exactly where is home, Aubrey? A lonely little apartment in New York, or some place where people need you and want you? Where you are important, not just another face in the crowd."

"Stop it."

"Stop what?"

"Quit trying to make me feel guilty for wanting to live the life I choose to live. I'll be gone... as soon as these casts come off and I can walk again."

He hesitated and his voice was quieter. "And is that what you really want?"

No, what I really want, I can't have. "Yes, it is."

His expression turned into a frown. Connor's eyes became subdued. The fire lighting them appeared to lose most of its luster. His gaze was no longer directed toward her. "I see. Gotta go. Don't want to be late picking Grey up." He turned away.

"Wait. Let me grab a jacket and I'll come with you."

"You don't need to. It's fine. I can pick her up myself."

Sadness filled her. *I've hurt him.* She wheeled over and touched his hand. "No, Connor. I want to be there, too." She tried to pull herself away, but her hand resisted. Almost as if he were a magnet and she were steel.

Connor's comment not only stung her, but interrupted the spell. "Why? We're not really important."

"That wasn't what I said. Look, it came out harsher than I meant it."

"I doubt that. I believe I read between the lines perfectly. And you're right, Aubrey."

"Right about what? I don't understand."

Connor walked to the door, opened it and then turned. "I had it all wrong. This *was* just a brief stop, only a place to recuperate. Goodbye." He grabbed his coat and reached for the door handle.

A kaleidoscope of images flashed before her. Of memories and dreams wanting to come true. Aubrey and Leslie shopping. Family meal times. Doing jigsaw puzzles with Mimes. Sitting next to Connor on the porch, watching the stars. Walks through the fields. Dancing in the rain. Holding hands while riding in a sleigh. Playing games with Grey. "Connor?"

He turned, eyes pale and near lifeless. "What?"

"I changed my mind. I want to be there for Grey. Let me tag along."

"You don't need to."

"Look, when I was younger, there were many times when I was hurting inside. Times I wanted someone to be there for me. Nights when I needed a friend, but no one cared and I cried myself to sleep. I can't let Grey go through this alone. I will be there for her."

He didn't move, but instead watched her face. There was something there she couldn't read. The distance between them seemed to shrink. And in his eyes, she noted a slight glimmer, as if something was trying to get out. An almost overwhelming desire to hug Connor was growing, but the enchantment was broken when he turned and retrieved her jacket from the peg. He held it out for her. "I'm here too, Aubrey. And believe it or not, I also care."

Connor stood behind her so he could guide the coat across her shoulders, but she could see his reflection in the glass on the door. And how his gaze took her in. *Were you just talking about Grey, or me, too?*

***

The autumn wind was brisk, bringing with it an earthy wood fire scent, even though Joe couldn't identify the source from his vantage point. He closed his eyes and the vision of a crackling fireplace filled his mind. The flames were reflected in the soft brown hues of Aubrey's eyes. She was sitting on his lap, so warm, so delightful. The beauty leaned down until their lips blended together. Her fingers grabbed his shirt and drew him even closer. Then, to his surprise, she...

"Joseph." Connor stood before him. His friend must have opened the door while Joe was daydreaming.

Joseph? "How've you been, buddy?" Joe extended his hand, but Connor just stood there. *Looking pissed.*

"What can I do for you?"

What did I do to make him angry? "I'm here to pick Aubrey up for our date."

Connor's jaw clenched and his eyes narrowed. He didn't move.

"Connor, why don't you ask Joe to come in?" Connor spun to face the source of the voice, his sister Leslie. Her next words were soft, but Joe picked up on them. "It's my house. He's a friend of our guest and Joe's welcome. Let him in."

Connor's face was red. "Leslie..."

She hissed her words. "No. Not... not now."

Connor nodded and then swung open the door. "Fine. Come in if you want."

What did I walk into? He'd never seen Connor act this way. Joe touched his friend's shoulder. "You okay?"

Connor glanced in his direction. His fists were curled. "Yeah, sure. I'm just peachy." He headed up the stairs without another word.

Joe shrugged and turned his attention to the two girls seated at the table. Connor's niece Grey had her back toward him. A tower of wooden blocks was precariously teetering between them. His eyes gravitated to the other girl. Aubrey smiled and wrinkled her nose. "Hello. As soon as I beat Grey in Jenga, I'll be ready. Is it your turn, Grey?"

"Nope. It's yours, Abs."

Aubrey nibbled at her lip while she contemplated her move. Finally, she used her index finger to gently slide one of the blocks slightly out of place. Aubrey grasped the wood between her fingers and pulled. As soon as it was free, the rest of the tower crumbled.

She frowned. "I thought I had this figured out."

The little girl reached for the storage bin sitting on the table. "I win, again." She handed the plastic box to the older woman. "Loser has to clean up."

Leslie walked over and took the container from Aubrey's hand. "I've got this. You have company."

"You sure?"

Leslie nodded.

"Thanks." Aubrey rolled her wheelchair from the table until she was in front of Joe. "Do I look good enough to go along with you tonight?"

A long pink skirt hid her casts. A dark blue cardigan sweater covered her shoulders, while a white turtleneck peeked out above it. Her curly hair shimmered under the dining room chandelier, accenting Aubrey's large, soft eyes. But the feature that caught his attention was those plump lips. *I can't wait to taste them.* They were covered in the same shade of pink as her dress. He swallowed hard. "You look ravishing tonight."

Her entire face broke into a smile. "Thanks. Let me grab my purse and I'll be ready."

"Abs?" Both Aubrey and Joe turned to focus on the girl.

The look of angst on Grey's face concerned Joe. Aubrey swiveled her chair to face the girl. "Yes?"

"Do you really hafta go?"

The curly-haired girl rolled over and hugged the little brunette. "Yes, but I'll be home later. Maybe, if Aunt Leslie lets you stay up, we can make popcorn and watch a movie together."

Grey clung to Aubrey. "Promise?"

"Cross my heart and hope to die."

"Okay. Love you, Abs." She hugged Aubrey and held on for a very long time.

Joe bid the other two ladies farewell after he helped Aubrey with her coat. The late afternoon sun was starting to wane. Joe assisted Aubrey into the car before stowing her wheelchair. Joe closed the door and turned to face her.

Aubrey smiled, and those gorgeous lips continued to tempt him. "I'm sorry about that."

"About what, Grey not wanting you to leave?"

She shook her head. "No. About the way Connor treated you."

"Yeah, what was he upset about?"

Aubrey hesitated before replying. "Me, and you."

***

The wind had picked up, spitting a cold drizzle from the darkening sky. Steam escaped in white wisps of vapor from around the pistons of the steam locomotive. Aubrey glanced over her shoulder. "Who did you say we're meeting?"

His brilliant white teeth complimented his All-American looks. "Two very good friends of mine, the Elliots."

A happy looking couple approached. The joy covering the woman's face removed all of Aubrey's anxiety. The lady extended her hand. "Hi. You must be Aubrey. Joe's told us so much about you." The girl giggled. "I'm Daisy Elliot and this is my Mr. Right, Jake."

"Mr. Right?"

Joe rubbed Aubrey's shoulder. Her skin tingled from the touch. "There's a long story behind the name."

"A long story?"

Daisy laughed. "Yes. I fell in love with Jake almost twenty years ago, when I was thirteen. I knew he was the one for me the day I met him." Her husband came and wrapped his arms around Daisy's waist.

Jake shook his head. "Daisy, she probably doesn't want to hear our tale."

Aubrey couldn't help but smile. "I don't know. This sounds interesting."

Joe chimed in. "Oh please, don't give her an opening. We'll have to listen to this for the entire train ride."

Daisy winked at Aubrey. "Joe's trying to change the subject. You know, Aubrey, he had a major part to play in Jake and I getting together."

"You don't say..." She glanced at Joe. "He played Cupid, huh? It seems there's a lot he hasn't told me."

The doctor's smile was ear to ear. "Yet. I plan on sharing everything with you and hope you'll pay me the same courtesy."

Aubrey had to glance away. There were certain things she'd never tell Joe or anyone else. A voice seemed to whisper in her ear. *Not even Connor?*

"Aubrey?"

She shook her head to shed the thought. "Sorry. Yes. In time."

The railroad conductor directed two other workers to bring a portable ramp to span the distance between the train platform and the dining car. The men were careful with their ward. Once she was back on a solid surface, Joe pushed the wheelchair into an elegant dining room. The woodwork was breathtaking, and the red velvet curtains looked as if they'd just been hung. Joe held her chair while she transferred to a deeply cushioned bench seat facing the window.

Daisy sat across from her. She held her husband's hand, but addressed Aubrey. "When we get to Paradise, maybe we can switch seats so you can check out the scenery on the other side of the track."

Jake laughed. "It's pretty country scenery, but the most beautiful sight is inside the train." He kissed his wife's fingers.

Aubrey sighed. "How long have you two been married?"

The train started moving. An attendant stopped by and filled their glasses with a pale wine. When he moved on to the next table, Daisy answered. "It will soon be two years."

Aubrey took a sip of her wine and hiccupped. "I'm sorry. Excuse me."

Joe patted her arm. "No worries. You're among friends."

Warmth slowly spread up Aubrey's arms. *The wine or the company?* "This is really nice. Thank you for asking me to tag along."

"My pleasure." He turned to Jake and Daisy. "Aubrey's an actress."

Daisy's eyes widened. "Wow. Were you on TV or in the movies?"

Aubrey quickly shook her head. "No. A couple of off-Broadway plays." She took another sip of her wine. "I had just landed a major supporting role on Broadway, but then I was in an accident."

Compassion filled Daisy's face. "What happened?"

Aubrey had to delay until the waiter delivered the cheese and grape tray. Aubrey took a cracker and a piece of Swiss cheese. "I got hit by a truck while crossing the street."

Jake's hand stopped before any food crossed his lips. "Did the driver run a red light?"

Aubrey grimaced as the accident replayed in her mind. "It was both our faults. He told the police it was stale yellow and I jumped the gun on crossing the light."

Daisy patted her hand. "How horrible. That must have been frightening."

"The worst part was the clown."

Both Jake and Daisy asked simultaneously, "Clown?"

Aubrey nodded. "The driver was dressed as a clown. He worked at a costume shop."

Jake cocked his head. "Do you still have the role, I mean when you are finished healing?"

"No. They simply moved on to the next actress."

Daisy took her hand. "You know, Aubrey, when God closes a door, He always opens a window. One thing I've found is that what comes next is often better than what was before."

Aubrey studied her new friend. "Sorry, Daisy. I'm not really a believer." *Especially now.*

Daisy paled, but squeezed her hand again. "That's okay. I didn't mean to offend you."

"You didn't. I just, uh, can we change the subject?"

Daisy rapidly nodded her head.

Joe let out a soft laugh. "Let's keep talking about your acting career."

A chill worked its way up her spine. "There wasn't much else."

"Really? That's not what I found when I Googled you."

The chill was replaced by searing heat in her face. *Please no.* "Y-you G-googled me? Don't always believe what it says on the internet."

"Really, Aubrey?" Joe winked, setting terror loose in her mind. "She's being modest." He leaned back and studied her. "You weren't totally honest with us. You do have film credits."

Oh no. The videos that were on my stolen phone. If she could have moved on her own, she would have run to the end of the car and jumped off. "I, I can explain."

Joe's smile terrified her. "Nothing to explain." He turned to Jake and Daisy. "Seems Aubrey starred

in a series of TV commercials for the public library."
He squeezed her hand. "I watched them. You looked
so cute."

Aubrey's pulse started to slow. *Forgot about
those.* "That, uh, they were nothing."

Her friend's smile increased. "I thought they
were really good. I might have to get your autograph
later."

Aubrey nodded and reached for her goblet. Her
hand was shaking so badly that the wine almost
topped the rim.

Daisy's eyebrows raised. "Are you okay, Aubrey?"

She was quick in her response. "Guess I was just
thinking about the... accident. Yeah, the accident. I
was, uh, on the way back from the library when I got
hit." *Please let him talk about something else.*

Joe patted her back. "We'll change the subject. I
didn't mean to bring up bad memories."

"Thanks." *And please don't Google me anymore.*

Chapter 12

The sound of coughing echoed up the stairs from the kitchen. Pushing the door open, Connor took a look at his sister. Her hair was messed up, her eyes and the area around her nose were dull red. "Hey, are you okay?"

"I think she's sick." Connor turned to find Aubrey sitting there. "And like always, too stubborn to allow anyone to help her. You know, no one can do it like the great Leslie Lapp."

Leslie coughed into her elbow. "I need to pack Grey's lunch and," she turned her head and sneezed, "I might as well make breakfast."

"You don't look well. Let me help, sis."

"It's no bother, really. I don't mind." She sneezed again. "I'm too busy to be sick."

Connor placed his hands on his hips as he stared at her. "There's two things I'm concerned about. One, with you spreading your germs all over the place, is that we're all going to catch whatever it is you have. But more importantly, I'm concerned about you. What's that phrase you always say to me? Oh, I remember. 'You need to take care of yourself first.' Did you forget or doesn't that apply to you?"

"I can't let a cold get me down. I've got too much going on this week. I need to finalize the plans for the Sunbury project today and then present my concept to their management team tomorrow." Leslie grabbed Connor's hand. "And we can't let Grey down. We promised to take her to Skyline Drive this weekend."

Connor groaned. Leslie could be so hard-headed when it came to things. "I could present the plans to the client."

Leslie sniffled and wiped her nose with a tissue. "No offense, but I think our chances are better if a woman does it."

"Why do you think that?"

"After some of the things they said, I get the distinct impression they prefer to work with diverse businesses."

Connor shook his head and raised a finger. But before he could say anything, Aubrey spoke up. "I'd like to pitch it for you."

The siblings spun to face her. Leslie addressed Aubrey. "I appreciate your willingness to help, but you're not familiar enough with the business."

"Then coach me. Give me a script to deliver. After all, I am an actress."

"Suppose they ask you a question you can't answer?"

Aubrey was momentarily silent. When she spoke, she avoided Connor's eyes. "In that case, I'll ask your brother. He's very knowledgeable. And even the top managers don't know everything. That's why you have a team. In this case, the best team I've ever seen. The Lapp Interior Design Team." She rolled closer to Leslie. "What do you think?"

Leslie stared at Aubrey, then turned to Connor. "What's your opinion?"

He glanced at Aubrey and she quickly looked away, avoiding his eyes. "It's worth a try, sis. You're in no shape to do it and I believe... no, I have total faith that Aubrey can do anything she sets her mind to."

Leslie threw her hands in the air. "Fine, fine. I can tell where I'm not wanted and I know a conspiracy when I see one." A smile suddenly graced her lips. "You were right, Aubrey."

Connor had to force himself not to laugh at the girl's expression. "Right about what?"

"What you said earlier."

Aubrey shrugged. "I don't understand."

When Leslie covered her mouth to cough, Connor continued. "About us, being a team. The best team. And Leslie and I are both glad you're on it."

Leslie smiled through her sniffles. "And so happy you came here. You're more than a team member. Aubrey, you're part of the family now. An important part."

Aubrey's expression melted, her face turned red and then she swiveled her chair so her back was toward them. She moved to the counter and grabbed a tissue from the box.

Connor shot a look at his sister. She shrugged.

"Is everything okay?" he asked. "Did we say something wrong?"

When Aubrey didn't move, Leslie walked to her friend. "What's the matter?"

To Connor's surprise, Aubrey grabbed hold of Leslie in a tight hug. Her voice was high when she spoke. "Thanks. I've never been part of a real family before."

***

"Why did I ever offer to do this?"

Connor raised his eyebrows as a precursor to that grin. The one that made her dizzy. An image appeared in her mind. Of sun shining through a window, igniting those blue eyes as his head lay on the pillow. The one next to hers. "You'll do great."

Aubrey frowned. "It's not like I have a script. Your sister was rather vague as to what I should say."

He laughed. "You'll have to forgive Leslie. She was sick."

Aubrey nodded. "Regardless, I'm ill-equipped and not as prepared as I thought I would be. I'm worried I'll fail."

"Don't underestimate yourself. Just do your best. That's all anyone can ask for. And if you get nervous, look at me."

"Why?"

"Because you can trust me."

Like when you took Marci back? "Just jump right in if I start to struggle."

A gentleman opened the glass door separating the lobby from the hallway. "Good morning. They're ready for you now."

She and Connor followed the man down a passageway. Aubrey was not impressed with what she surveyed around her. The floor tiles were uneven and, in some cases, broken. The diffusers on the overhead light fixtures were yellowed with age. The few wall hangings were random. Glancing into an office she passed, the heavy steel file cabinets appeared to have been built to withstand a nuclear attack. And the massive gray desk seemed weary, as if it had seen much better days and was waiting to retire.

The man directed them into a conference room with a large wooden table. He then removed a chair to make a place for Aubrey, but the table design wouldn't allow her to scoot close. And because of the number of people at the table, Connor had to stand. Behind her.

It only took Connor a few minutes to set up the computer and projector. When he reached around to place the show books in front of her, Connor whispered in her ear. "Piece of cake, Aubrey. And never forget, I believe in you."

Aubrey closed her eyes briefly. *Please, if You're there, help me to do well.* She took a second to contemplate what she'd just done. She'd said a prayer to someone she didn't believe existed.

The man who had escorted them to the room introduced the individuals sitting around the table before departing. As always when she took the stage, Aubrey felt the transformation begin, turning from herself into the character she was playing. A smile graced her lips. *I've got this.*

"Good morning and thank you for your time. Leslie Lapp is a bit under the weather today and I volunteered to step up to the plate. My name is Aubrey Stettinger and I'm her assistant." She pivoted and introduced Connor. From there, her instincts took over. Thoughts and words she didn't think she knew seemed to flow from her lips. And as often happened when she was on stage, her audience became mesmerized.

The time flew past. She glanced at the clock in the waiting area on their way out. Almost three hours had passed.

Connor was quiet until they were both seated in his truck and her chair was stowed. He turned to her. "Wow. I think *I* learned a few things about interior design while listening to you. And the passion you had when you were giving your spiel, amazing."

Aubrey felt her cheeks heat. "Stop it. I didn't really do much."

He shook his head. "Well, from my vantage point, you did very well." Even though her attention was focused on the scenery passing outside the passenger window, she could sense his eyes were on her. "So did Leslie coach you to say it?"

Aubrey couldn't resist. She turned to him. "Say what?"

He grinned, raising her body temperature a bit. "How did you put it? 'The Lapp Interior Design Team is the best I've ever seen. Completely driven by honest values, highest quality and the relentless pursuit of excellence. And I'm honored to be part of this team.' Where'd that come from?"

She had to look away. "It's the truth. You guys are great. I've never known anyone like the two of you. Such a great team." *I'm going to miss this.*

He touched her arm. "Thanks, but you forgot one. There's not just two on the team, but three." She couldn't meet his eyes. "It's lunch time. Let's celebrate. Want to grab something here or closer to home?"

"I'm okay to wait to eat, but I could use a drink."

Aubrey was lost in her thoughts as Connor drove them out of Shamokin Dam to the highway. The trees were past their peak, but a few remnants of color remained. A warmth filled her. *I've never been more at peace with myself than I am right now.*

Connor seemed to sense she was tired and remained quiet. But his presence comforted her. The rhythm of the wheels lulled her to the brink of slumber, whispering the words... *This, this is where you belong.*

***

Connor closed the door after checking on Leslie. She had a fever now. He descended the stairs.

"How is she?" Aubrey was at the bottom of the steps wearing a dress. A soft red shade of gloss covered her lips and gave them the appearance of being wet. He had to stifle his desire to taste them.

"Not well. I need to make a doctor's appointment for her. I'm wondering if she has the flu."

"Isn't it a bit early in the year for that?"

He shrugged. "Maybe, I don't know. But I don't believe you have a temperature with a cold."

Grey looked up from the table, where she was doing her homework. "Does this mean we're not going away this weekend?"

He walked over and hugged his niece. "Of course we will. But we'll have to see how Aunt Leslie's feeling. It might just be you and me."

The little girl frowned. "That doesn't sound like fun. Just us two."

Ouch. "I'll try to make it a wonderful time. A great memory."

"Can Mimes come?"

"She has a bus trip on Saturday, remember?"

Grey concentrated on her paper. She suddenly stood and turned to Aubrey. "Can you come, Abs? It'll be fun. I really want you to."

Connor's eyes moved to Aubrey. Her face was bright red. "I, uh, don't know."

Grey walked over and took Aubrey's hand. "I want you to come."

"Grey, let me talk to Uncle Connie for a few minutes." Her eyes motioned toward the kitchen. She rolled in and he followed. Inside the kitchen, she spun the chair around and faced him. "Where exactly are you going?"

Connor sat down. "We're leaving Friday morning. Going down Skyline Drive to take in the trees, then spending the night in Luray, Virginia. Saturday, we'll drive to the Natural Bridge, and Sunday we can visit one of the Smithsonian museums in D.C." She didn't look too happy. "Hey, maybe Leslie will make a recovery before then."

"That seems like an awful lot of driving."

"We could make lots of stops along the way."

Aubrey was concentrating on her hands. "And what about the sleeping arrangements?"

"That's going to depend."

Aubrey's eyes opened wide and she pushed her chair away from him. "D-depends on what?"

"Who's going. Leslie and Grey were going to share a room by themselves, but if it's just Grey and me, I'll cancel one of the reservations. Why'd you ask?"

Aubrey ignored his question and glanced at her phone. "It's getting late. Joe will soon be here."

So that's why you're dressed up. "Okay. Look, don't worry about it. If Leslie is still sick, Grey and I will make it a twosome." *What could you possibly see in Joe?* "We'll manage."

Connor turned toward the door. The sadness in her words stopped him. "I remember what it was like. I can't let her down."

He turned to her. Aubrey's eyes were watery. "What it was like? What do you mean?"

"The loneliness of childhood. Needing someone, but nobody really cared. That little girl is going through some really tough times. She needs a friend. Like it or not, I have to be there for her."

Like it or not? The meaning behind those words cut deep. "Don't feel forced into something you don't want to do. Maybe Leslie will recover."

She wasn't looking at him. "I doubt she'll feel up to it. Grey needs a woman to be with her."

"So her uncle's company isn't enough?"

Her eyes shifted and engaged him. The glare was enough to melt steel. "This is not about you, Connor Lapp. This is about Greiston. She's what's important here." Aubrey rolled forward until she was close enough to touch. "You have no idea what it is like to grow up in a broken home. From what you've shared, your childhood was filled with love. Hers is not. You can't comprehend the loneliness, the pain of seeing your parents fight or the guilt you blame on yourself. I can't and won't let her down."

He could see and feel her fury. Her anger. Her desire to protect his niece. But there was one thing she didn't see. The way she looked. *You're even more beautiful when you're inspired.* "Then I guess it's decided? You're coming?"

He could physically see her defiance fade. She motioned for him to step aside, then turned her attention to the floor. "Like I have a choice."

***

Joe smiled at the lady with the long curly locks. "You look absolutely breathtaking this evening, Aubrey."

A deep blush slowly blossomed from her neck to her cheeks. "Thank you. This restaurant is very elegant, but the food is really expensive."

They were at the Log Cabin restaurant in Leola. "Don't worry about the cost. It's well worth it and besides, being with you is priceless."

After they ordered, the waiter delivered a bread basket. Joe noted Aubrey was very quiet tonight. Not only that, but she didn't look him in the eyes. "Did I do something wrong?"

She nibbled her bread and shook her head. Aubrey washed down the food with a sip of water. "No. Not at all."

Joe waited, but she didn't continue. "Something's bothering you. What is it?"

She looked everywhere except at him. Joe could see her swallow hard just before she met his gaze. The flames from the restaurant's fireplace were reflected in her soft brown eyes "I've, uh, got to break our date Friday night."

"That's not a problem. Want to do Saturday instead?"

Aubrey slowly shook her head. "I can't."

The small hairs on the back of his neck stood on end. "Are you sure I didn't do something wrong?"

Her hand found his. He was surprised at how cold it was. Joe's fingers instinctively wrapped around hers. She tilted her head slightly, a frown covering those beautiful lips. "I have something I need to do this weekend. I hate to break our plans and I don't want you to think..." Her eyes dropped as her voice trailed off.

"Don't want me to think... what?"

She pulled her hand from his, but teased his palm with her index finger as she lazily traced figure eights on it. "That you're not important to me."

Warmth grew in his chest. "Am I important to you?"

She looked down. *Her blush is back.* "I hope you know you are."

Joe felt his lips curl. "Oh, yeah?" The urge to tease her overtook him. "So does this mean you like me?"

Aubrey's eyes softened. Joe's heart started to melt. "Yes, very much."

"I really care for you, too." *It's more than liking you. A lot more.* He was struggling for the right words to say when the waiter arrived.

"Here are your steaks. Please check to make sure they're done just right."

Joe sliced into his filet. "Mine's great. How is yours... honey?"

Aubrey's eyes widened and those plump lips were working hard to contain the smile. "Perfect, just like you... sweetheart."

Even though they ate in silence, quite a few happy looks were shared. That changed right after dessert was ordered. "So what do you have going on this weekend?"

Aubrey swallowed hard. "I'm taking a trip."

"Really? Where are you going?"

"Virginia. I told you about Grey's parents and the problems that poor little girl is going through."

The warmth that had been in his chest for the past hour started to cool. "And that means?"

"Leslie was going to take her away for the weekend, but she came down with the flu. So I'm filling in."

"Why do you need to fill in for her?"

Aubrey's eyes were concentrating on her hands. "My childhood wasn't the best. I've been exactly where Grey is at now. No one cared enough to make a difference in my life." She tilted her head so they could clearly see each other. "I will not let that precious little child go through this alone."

Joe's heart filled with pride. "You're something else. Putting another's needs ahead of yours. You are filled with compassion, such a pure heart. I'm glad we met."

Her eyes now clouded. "Me too. But there's one problem with this weekend."

"What's that?"

"Don't be mad at me. This part wasn't my choice. Guess who's taking Grey and me to Virginia?"

Chills ran rampant down his spine and his vision turned red. "No, not him."

Aubrey sighed and frowned. "Yep. You guessed it."

Chapter 13

C onnor slid the last of their belongings in the bed of his pickup, under the tonneau cover. "Okay, we're set. Let's saddle up."

Grey yawned. "Why do we hafta get up so early?"

He tousled her hair. "Like they say, the early bird gets the worm."

"I don't like worms. Do you, Abs?"

Aubrey's hair was pulled back this morning. Sleep was in her eyes. *Serves you right for staying out so late.*

Aubrey stretched. "I only like the gummy ones." She turned to Connor. "I think I might take a nap while you drive. Can you wake me when we stop for breakfast?"

Even though she looked tired and wasn't wearing makeup, Aubrey was still adorable. And, just like she predicted, she was asleep before he reached the Lincoln Highway. Glancing over, Grey was snuggled against Aubrey and they were both out.

Driving on in silence, Connor watched the colors come to life as the sun rose. The trees in York and Adams counties were past their peak. A good many of the homes they rolled by were decorated for Halloween. A sinking feeling grew in his heart as he replayed the conversation he'd overheard between Leslie and Aubrey the previous day.

He dropped the TV remote and was on his knees, looking for it. Aubrey's voice caught his attention from the kitchen. "I made an appointment for next week. These awful casts are finally coming off."

Leslie sneezed before responding. "When's your appointment? I'll take you."

"Joe volunteered to do it. I can't wait to walk on my own again."

He picked up on the sadness in his sister's voice. "Then what?"

"Joe told me it will take a couple of weeks to build up my strength again. After I do, I'll be heading back to New York City."

"I see. I hope you don't rush it. We've kind of gotten used to you hanging around. You're an important part of our family now and..."

"Please, let's not go there. I appreciate you and all the kindness you've given me. There will be plenty of chances to be sad later. Let's just enjoy the time we still have."

Connor turned his head to take in the sight. Grey was snuggled tightly against her. Aubrey looked so beautiful, sitting on the seat, head resting against his niece. *I can't let her go. Lord, help me to find some way to change her heart, to make her want to stay.*

He slid his truck into a space in the parking lot off of Steinwehr Avenue near the restaurant. Aubrey began to stir. A warm smile formed as her eyes opened. "Where are we? Wait, I know this place. Leslie took me here for lunch." Aubrey looked around before facing him again. "This is Gettysburg, right?"

"Yep. Ready for breakfast?"

She studied him for a long moment. "This is nice, taking Grey on this trip. I know how busy you are. You're a good man, Connor."

He wanted to slide across the seat and hold her, but Grey was there between them. "We're making memories she'll have for a lifetime. But I'm pretty sure the thing she'll remember most is that you were there for her. You're special, Aubrey."

Her smile changed a little and was now sad. "Thanks for saying that, but it's not true. Grey's the one who's special. So smart and pretty. If I'm lucky, maybe someday I'll have a daughter like her." Her lips turned into a frown and she inhaled slowly through her nose. "Promise me you'll watch over her after I'm gone. I feel bad for what she's going through."

"You've been a godsend for her. She needs you." *But not as much as I do.* "Aubrey, I overheard you and Leslie talking about what will happen when your casts come off. About you going back to..." Aubrey held up her finger for him to be quiet as the child began to stir.

Grey lazily stretched her arms and opened her eyes. "Where are we?"

Aubrey gently kissed her head. "Good morning, sweetie. We're in Gettysburg. Are you hungry?"

The girl nodded. "I want chocolate chip pancakes. How 'bout you?"

"Hmm. I think I'll order bacon and eggs. What about Uncle Connie? What should we order for him?"

"He likes sausage gravy and potatoes."

What? Like I'm not even here? "Excuse me, ladies. Can I at least see what they have on the menu first?"

Aubrey shook her head. "Nope. You said this weekend was for Grey, so if she says you get sausage gravy, then that's what you'll get."

Grey giggled when Aubrey winked at her. "I like her, Uncle Connie."

He shook his head. "I can see this is going to be a long weekend for me. Shall we go in?"

Aubrey looked away. "You two go ahead. I'll catch up in a few minutes. I need to make a phone call first."

Connor stared at her. "It's seven-thirty. Who would you be calling at this hour?"

Those pretty plump lips turned into a smirk. "I don't believe that's any of your business, Mr. Lapp."

***

The buttery scent of the microwave popcorn didn't do much for Aubrey this evening. Especially considering their meal, the banana split she'd shared with Grey and the busy day they'd had. Her mind momentarily took her back to the beauty of the colors of the trees passing by and the awesome views of the valley below. After Skyline Drive, Connor had taken them to Luray Caverns. Today was the first time she and Grey had ever been inside a cave. The splendor of the rock formations had moved her.

"Moana will be ready when we are." Of course, Connor was talking about the movie he'd slipped into the media player. Ever prepared, he'd brought it along so Grey could watch her favorite shows on the road. Aubrey opened her eyes and took Connor in. So handsome, so tall, but those beautiful baby blues weren't glowing tonight. And he wasn't making eye contact with her either.

"I'm ready, Uncle Connie." The words somehow escaped between munches of popcorn. *It was a happy day for her*. The little girl deserved it.

Connor shook his head and then pulled his cell from his pocket. "Before we turn on the movie, we need to call Aunt Leslie. You need to tell her all about today. I know she really wanted to be here."

"Okay. Can we Facetime her?"

"Sure, baby."

He dialed his sister and passed the phone to the little girl after the call was answered. While Grey divulged all the goings on of the day to Leslie, Connor sat on a chair. He seemed focused on one of the paintings in the room. Aubrey swiftly transferred to her wheelchair and went to him. Something had changed with him and she was pretty sure she knew what it was.

"That painting seems to be quite interesting. Checking out the competition?"

He didn't look at her. "No. Just tired."

Connor had exerted a lot of energy, especially at the caverns. *He was so kind, pushing me up and down those inclines.* "I can see why you would be, but is that all? You seem down."

He laughed and his gaze dropped to study the carpet. "You know me well." She expected he would continue, but Connor remained silent.

Yes, I do. "You can talk to me."

"I know, but..."

He was holding something back. "But what?"

Grey suddenly burst out in laughter, drawing his attention. Leslie had made her laugh. "It's not important." Connor ran his hand through his hair.

Aubrey touched his arm. "It must be. I don't think I've ever seen you this down. Are you upset about something that happened today?"

He pursed his lips together. "No. I'm just thinking about that little girl and how her life is going to change."

"What do you mean?"

For the first time, Connor sought her eyes. "Leslie gave me the bad news today."

A strange tingling crossed her shoulders. "What news?"

"About her mom."

"Did something happen?"

He nodded. "Lisa and her boyfriend called Leslie from Las Vegas." The color of his eyes darkened. "My sister got remarried. She told Leslie they'll be living in Bakersfield."

"Bakersfield, as in California?"

He nodded. "Then she asked Leslie if Grey could stay with us until the end of the school year. That girl's world is about to be torn apart." He wiped his hand across his face. "I have no idea how to help her or what to do."

And then I'll be leaving. "What can I do?"

A fire appeared in his eyes. "Maybe you could..." His voice drifted off.

"Abs. Aunt Leslie wants to talk to you. Uncle Connie, can we start the movie?"

"No, we should wait for Aubrey."

She shook her head. "Go ahead and start it. I'll catch up in a few minutes." She rolled over and took the phone. "I'll go into the bathroom so I don't disturb you two."

Grey jumped on the king-sized bed and patted the spot next to her. "Here, Uncle Connie." Connor moved from the chair to the bed. Aubrey cast one last glance at the pair before closing the door. Grey had climbed onto his lap. She was so sweet, so innocent.

Aubrey whispered, "Wish I could do more to help her." To her surprise, it seemed a voice from behind her answered. *"You know what you could do."* Quickly spinning around, there was no one there.

***

The closing credits were rolling on the screen. Grey had fallen asleep about halfway through the movie. Her head was on Aubrey's lap, her feet across Connor's legs. Aubrey had also dozed off. Connor clicked the remote to power off the player. He smiled at the soft rhythmic breathing of both girls. *In the company of angels.*

Grey had enjoyed the day, which was exactly what all three adults had hoped for. Connor was glad Aubrey had come along. The pair had carried on, at times so engrossed in each other's company that

Connor wondered why he was even there. *There was a time when I was Grey's favorite person.* That had changed when Aubrey arrived. The bond between Grey and Aubrey had grown quick and deep.

Grey shifted slightly. Connor gently lifted her and repositioned the girl next to Aubrey. He tucked the covers tightly under her chin and kissed her hair. The scent of popcorn lingered and he noted the yellow at the corners of her mouth from the butter. "Good night, Grey. Don't let the bedbugs bite."

He continued to study the child. *What was wrong with Lisa?* His oldest sister had always been the wild child of the Lapp family. And she'd always lived her life just the way *she* wanted, never caring what others thought. Until last year, when she landed a good job with the state. But now Lisa was back to her old self, probably not realizing or giving a damn that her decision would tear her daughter's world apart. *My sister is selfish.* He whispered again to Grey, "I love you, little one."

Connor's gaze drifted to Aubrey. And what effect would her departure have on Grey? Losing both a mother and best friend was going to be devastating. His eyes rolled out of focus into a daydream. Of Aubrey never leaving. Of this beauty holding his hand as they walked through the journey of life, together. Strolls on the beach, discussing the shapes in the clouds, dancing under a full moon. *But that won't happen.* He and Aubrey had been so close, until that day he faltered, when Connor gave in to Marci's request for a second chance. And like a fool, he'd played right into his ex-girlfriend's hand.

Connor pried his attention from the two of them. He disconnected and packed the disc and player away. Glancing at his watch, he saw the night was still young enough to call Leslie. Hearing her voice would help. Lord above, he needed a friend right now.

"Honey?" He turned quickly at the sound of Aubrey's voice. Walking to the bed, he could see Aubrey's eyes were closed but her head was turning side to side. "Sweetheart?"

She was dreaming. *Of me?* He made sure to keep his voice low. "I'm right here."

A slight smile filled her lips. "Can you pass the brown sugar?"

Brown sugar? It dawned on him. Was she thinking about the tea room? Aubrey had been fascinated with the brown sugar cubes. That day had been magical. He played along. "Here you go."

Her right eyebrow raised for half a second. "Thanks. The grape jelly is sweet. Want to try it?"

The sudden desire to hold her, to kiss her moved him closer. Involuntarily, he leaned down until his face was close enough to feel her breath. Those lips looked so delicious. He couldn't wait any longer as he closed his eyes and... It was as if someone slapped him. *Stop this. It's not right.*

Chills ran down his back. *What am I doing?* She wasn't even awake. Connor gently lifted her and moved her to a more relaxed position. The warmth of her body in his arms raised his pulse. *I need to leave, now.* For his own sanity. His fingers moved the locks from her face before he tucked the covers up to her chin.

She rolled onto her side, facing him. "Let's walk in the creek." Aubrey had told him about this part of her life. From before her mother married the preacher. It was one of the few happy memories she'd shared from her childhood. On hot Sunday afternoons, Aubrey and her mom would sometimes go to the edge of town and splash around in the creek.

Funny. Connor had known this girl for such a short period of time, yet inside, it felt like it had been forever. His body ached to hold her, to sweep Aubrey off the bed, spin her around and kiss her.

Connor tensed and shook his head. *I need to quit this torture.* It was time to head to his room. Still, he couldn't resist. Leaning down, his lips brushed her forehead. "G'night, Aubrey. Sweet dreams."

Her expression didn't change. He turned to go when he heard Aubrey mumble, "You too... Joe."

Chapter 14

T he wind had picked up, sending a chill down Aubrey's back. She tugged the leather coat tighter. Connor's coat. She hadn't anticipated such a drastic temperature change and her light fleece wasn't enough to keep the cold from chilling her. But Connor had noticed her shiver that morning as they left the hotel. Without a word, he'd removed his jacket and draped it across her shoulders. His action added to the mounting feelings growing inside her. The one that whispered to her heart that she'd made a mistake. *Maybe he's not like Piotr.*

"Can we get some hot chocolate?" Grey was tugging on her arm. They had stopped at a little roadside market. Baskets of apples and bright orange pumpkins gave color to the dilapidated stand.

"I wonder if they have a restroom I can use."

Connor answered, "They do. When I mapped out the route, I made sure to pick stops that were wheelchair accessible."

Aubrey glanced at him. His eyes were empty, as they'd been all day. *He's upset about Grey.* Connor was so thoughtful.

"That was nice, planning ahead for me."

He shrugged his shoulders and then picked up a funny shaped gourd to examine. It had a green bottom and a yellow top.

Aubrey had never seen him like this. "You okay?"

"The new normal, I guess," He dropped the gourd and moved away from her.

"Uncle Connie, I'm hungry. Can I have some candy?"

Connor turned and knelt down so he was face to face with his niece. "Just one small piece. We don't want to spoil your appetite for supper."

Aubrey shook her head. He was a pushover when it came to the girl. Grey had him wrapped around her little finger. Aubrey entered the conversation. "I think you've had enough candy for one day, little miss."

Grey turned to face Aubrey with her lip stuck out. "Uncle Connie said I could have some." Connor was standing now, watching Grey. The little girl grabbed his hand and yanked, as if she were pulling the string to an old time school bell. "Can I have a candy bar? Please?"

He didn't even bother to look at her. "If Aubrey said no, then that's the answer."

"But you said yes first."

He nodded. "I did, but we should listen to Aubrey. Ladies are always smarter than men, so what she says goes. But I *will* buy you a cup of hot chocolate." His eyes now had a sadness to them and they were on Grey, not her. "Do you want one, too?"

Aubrey had let him down. She'd countered what he'd told Grey. *That wasn't right.* "I think I would."

Her gaze shifted from Connor to Grey. "I was wrong, Grey. Why don't you pick out a candy bar? I shouldn't have contradicted your uncle."

Grey's face lit up like sunshine. A deep contrast to the man standing next to her. His eyes seemed focused on the horizon as he held the door open. Aubrey followed Grey inside, pausing in front of him. "Sorry. That was wrong of me."

He didn't even look at her. "Don't worry about it."

After Aubrey had freshened up, she wheeled herself outside. A couple of picnic tables were on the right and there sat Connor and Greiston. The girl was finishing up an Almond Joy bar. "Hey, guys. How's the candy?"

Grey replied, though she was chewing. "Yummy." She handed Aubrey the spent candy wrapper, which had two chocolatey lumps on it. "Saved the nuts for you." Aubrey smiled because she knew what was coming. The line Grey always said when she gave Aubrey nuts. "'Cause you're crazy like a nut. How 'bout it, Uncle Connie?"

Aubrey giggled and transferred her gaze to the tall man sitting there. The one in a thin Millersville sweatshirt. "Do you think I'm crazy, Connor?"

He was delayed on his response. "That's not an adjective I'd attribute to you."

"Oh. What word would you use to describe me?"

He ignored the question and removed the lid to his Styrofoam cup. "I got cold apple cider. Want to try it, Grey?"

The girl quickly took the cup, uttering, "Um-hmm." She took a big sip. "That's good. Try it, Abs."

"Uh, no. That's your uncle's."

Connor shook his head. "I didn't drink out of it, so it's safe. Try it."

Safe? From what? Aubrey took a swig. The sweet liquid had a slight tang. As she swirled it around in her mouth, she tried to read Connor. *Nothing.* Stoic as a rock. "Thanks. It's really good."

Grey drew her attention. "Did you pick a word?"

Connor's eyebrows furrowed. "For what?"

"You know, about Abs."

For the first time in what seemed years, his eyes touched hers. A vision slowly appeared. Of Aubrey and Connor walking hand in hand down a path in an autumn wood. It faded when he stood and then drained his cup. "One word?"

Grey was dancing around, probably from too much sugar. "Yep."

Connor's eyes again found hers briefly. He uttered one solitary word before walking away. "Perfect."

***

His chest ached. *This is torture.* Sitting on the same seat as Aubrey, but knowing it would never be. No holding hands. No snuggling. No future together. Aubrey's actions had made that plain. She'd be gone in a couple of weeks and he'd never see her again.

He snuck a glance in her direction. Grey was asleep, but the woman was watching him. When Aubrey saw him turn his head, her smile broke out. "What a fun day. Thanks for taking me along."

Connor grunted and turned his attention back to the highway. Their exit was coming up. He lifted the turn signal.

"You're awfully quiet today. Penny for your thoughts."

"Just tired, I guess."

"Are you sure?"

He nodded his head. "Yep."

"You're fibbing. I can see what's going on. You wear your heart on your sleeve."

Then you can see it's broken. "No clue what you're talking about."

"And it's adorable."

Connor accelerated to pass a tanker in the slow lane. "Quit talking in riddles, please."

Aubrey laughed. "Fine. The way you care, the compassion and empathy you exhibit... it's touching. Like no one I've ever met. I think you're a great man, Connor Lapp."

Just not as good as the distinguished Joseph L. Rohrer, M.D. There was so much Connor wanted to say, but those words would never leave his lips. Instead, he muttered, "Thanks."

Dusk was lurking on the horizon. Clouds behind them blocked the setting sun. It was a bleary day. To top it off, the first wisps of a cold drizzle began to speckle the windshield. Aubrey's voice again interrupted his pity party. "Where were you thinking about stopping for supper?"

Connor hadn't slept well last night and was very tired. "I'd like to check in at the hotel first. There's a lot of restaurants in the..."

From the corner of his eye, he caught the movement. A deer suddenly materialized from out of the trees on the berm not far ahead. The buck wasn't in a hurry as it scampered across the road, directly in front of them.

Connor slammed on the brakes with both feet. Because he was in the passing lane, there was no place to go. He steered his skidding truck toward the median.

The tractor trailer behind them couldn't get stopped as quickly and was forced to swerve into the slow lane. The driver guided his behemoth expertly past their vehicle, mere inches between them.

Connor gripped the wheel tightly, waiting for the contact. To his right, Aubrey tightly wrapped Grey in her arms and turned her eyes from the road. In front of them, the eight-point buck gracefully leapt across the railing just in time. They had been close enough that Connor could see the individual hairs on the deer's legs.

Before any of them could breathe a sigh of relief, the squeal of locked tires and the blaring warning from the horn of an approaching truck forced his attention to the rearview. The grill of a huge Kenworth grew large in the mirror as it bore down on them.

Please put your arms around us. Protect Grey and Aubrey.

Connor floored the accelerator as the massive rig bore down on them. It was so close he could no longer see the headlights in the mirror.

The rear of Connor's truck fishtailed as he clung to the steering wheel. After what seemed to be minutes, the steel-belted radials found traction and thrust the Chevy away from certain destruction. The front of the huge diesel behind him was finally becoming smaller in the distance.

Thank You, God, for protecting us.

"Are you two alright?" His voice was squeaky.

There was no answer. He chanced a glance their way. Aubrey's face was deathly pale. "You just saved our lives, Connor." He reached for her and she gripped his hand tightly. "Thank you. I think we're alright, aren't we, Grey?"

The little girl's voice was high. "I need to pee."

Just ahead in the distance, there was a sign detailing food and fuel options available at the upcoming turnoff. His hand trembled as he tried to pull it from Aubrey, but her grip tightened momentarily. She gave his hand one more long, tight squeeze before finally releasing it. "Maybe we should all take a few minutes to compose ourselves."

Connor lifted the turn signal and headed for the exit. "Okay. Great idea."

Her voice was soft when she spoke again. "You're a hero."

He shook his head. "No, I'm not."

When she didn't answer, he turned to her. In the darkening gloom, the brilliance of her teeth reflected in the lights of passing cars. "For the second time in my life, you've saved me from harm. And yes, you are a hero, Connor Lapp. *My* hero."

***

Aubrey studied her reflection in the mirror. The warmth in her chest was about to make her blood boil. *Who am I trying to kid?* The attraction was strong to both men, Joe and Connor. While Joe was very kind and more eye-catching, Connor was the one who set her heart aflame. *I was so wrong about Connor.* She knew it was his compassion that caused him to give Marci a second chance, not some stupid game like she'd imagined.

"Abs, are you coming? I'm starved." Grey's face must have been against the door.

"Be out in a minute, sweetie." Maybe it was time to open back up to him, to give romance a shot before she left. *I love it here. I really want to stay.* For the first time ever, she felt like she was part of a real family.

There was a banging on the door. "Abs!"

"Coming." Aubrey shot a parting glance at the mirror. The woman smiling back looked confident. She admired the gloss on her lips. She hoped he'd notice. *I put it on for you, Connor.*

When Aubrey opened the door, Grey almost fell into the room. Aubrey had to giggle. "Okay, my little jack in the box, where do you want to go for dinner?"

"I want to go to that place you told me about. You know, the one where they put on a show when they cook?"

"Oh, I think you mean a hibachi restaurant."

Grey touched Aubrey's face. "Your lips look wet. Can you put some of this on me?"

"You might be a little too young for lipstick. So, have you ever eaten Japanese food before?"

"I dunno. What do they eat?"

Aubrey lifted the girl to her lap, grabbed her purse and wheeled to the door. The room in this hotel had an automatic door, which swung open slowly after Aubrey depressed the button. "Japanese people eat pretty much the same things we do, but they prepare it differently. And at the hibachi, they'll make rice and vegetables and whatever kind of meat you want. What are you hungry for?"

Grey didn't even take time to think. "Shrimpees."

"That sounds like an excellent idea. I'll have the same."

By the time Aubrey wheeled into the lobby, Connor was there. His smile seemed forced and Aubrey guessed why. *Still nervous from the near accident.* The poor guy looked so tired. He knelt down so his face was level with Grey's. "Where do you want to go for dinner?"

"A Japanese library."

He laughed. "What?"

Aubrey tried, but failed to stifle her laughter when he offered a look of confusion. "She means a hibachi."

"Oh, that makes more sense." As Grey sat on Aubrey's lap, Connor pushed them both to the truck. He nodded at Aubrey. "Can you pull up the directions on your phone?"

"I'd love to. Do you realize we make a great team, the three of us?" Connor's eyes questioned her comment, but she only smiled.

His gaze dropped to her lips and remained there for a few seconds. "Nice lip gloss. Makes your lips glisten and look wet."

Grey shook her head. "They're not. Touch them, Uncle Connie."

Aubrey felt her face heat. Connor's cheeks turned bright red and he looked away.

Connor was quiet as he drove along, but he kept glancing at her. With Aubrey's directions, they reached the restaurant in just a few minutes. She couldn't help but notice not only his strength, but the warmth of his breath as he lifted her out of the cab. A rush of air escaped her chest when Grey jumped on her lap.

The hostess seated the three of them on one side of the grill, and then brought in additional patrons to fill all the chairs.

The scent of grilled meat was mouthwatering, whetting Aubrey's appetite. After the waitress had collected the other diners' orders, she moved on to Aubrey. "What would you like?"

"Oh, shrimp, of course."

"White or brown rice?"

Aubrey turned to Grey. "How about I order brown rice and you order white? We'll split it so you can try both. Okay?"

Grey nodded in agreement. "Order for me, Abs." Aubrey did.

Connor was the last to order. "I'll take the steak."

"How would you like it cooked?"

"Well done, and may I make a request?"

"Yes."

"Can you cook my steak away from the seafood?"

The waitress nodded and walked away.

Grey pulled at Aubrey's sleeve. "Where's the show?"

Aubrey touched her nose. "The chef will put it on. Just wait."

Her eyes drifted past Grey, to the man seated next to the child. She'd felt him watching her ever since they sat down. While there seemed to be a question in his eyes, it was much different than earlier. It seemed as if he was probing her and her intentions.

Instead of avoiding him, this time she met his gaze and gave him what she hoped was an award-winning smile. For the first time since they'd left on Friday morning, his lips curled into a genuine smile.

Grey yanked her sleeve, breaking Aubrey's concentration. "Look, Abs. Is that the cook?"

The young oriental man sported a dark mustache which was immaculately trimmed. Grey was mesmerized with his act. When he sliced the onion into rings, built a volcano and ignited the liquid he'd squirted inside, Grey laughed and clapped her hands with glee.

Connor seemed his old self as he teased not only Grey, but Aubrey, too. It felt so good to hear him laugh. Her mind happily recalled the closeness they'd shared before Marci drove the wedge between them.

All too soon, the chef doled out the meat and veggies on plates. Grey grabbed her fork and was about to harpoon a shrimp when Connor stopped her. "Young lady! Where are your manners? You're forgetting to say a prayer of thanks for the food."

Grey acted so grown up when she returned her fork to the table and reached for the hands of both adults. Much to Aubrey's surprise, Connor offered his left hand to Aubrey. She willingly took it and felt his warmth flow into her as their fingers entwined. She squeezed his hand tightly only to have him reciprocate. At the end of Grey's prayer, she raised her chin. Connor sported the biggest smile she'd ever seen. Warmth started in her core, then flowed to her limbs.

"Are your shrimpees good, Grey?"

"Um-hmm."

His eyes landed on her. Aubrey had to look away. "And how's your meal, Abs?" She swallowed extra hard to force the food down. That was the first time he'd expressed that term of endearment in like, forever. *So good to hear you call me that.*

"Scrumptious. How's yours?"

He didn't answer right away. When she glanced in his direction, Connor's face was pale. He was digging through his rice and vegetables with his fork. Connor speared a chunk that looked like onion and examined it. He held it up for her to see. "Does that look like shrimp?"

"Yes."

His hands started to tremble and he dropped the utensil. The fork clinked loudly when it struck the plate, drawing the attention of everyone at the table. Connor yanked his jacket from the back of the chair. His eyes grew wild as he frantically searched for something in his pocket. "What's wrong?"

He pulled his car keys free, then turned to Grey. "I need you to do something right away."

Grey turned to him as she chewed a mouthful of food. "What, Uncle Connie?"

"In the glove box of my truck, grab my emergency needle. Remember which one that is?"

Aubrey was confused at the look of horror on the girl's face. "Are you okay?"

His words were slurring. "Hurry, Grey, please."

His niece ripped the keys from his hand and ran from the dining room. Aubrey turned her head back to Connor. He was violently scratching his mid-section. "Connor, you're scaring me. What's going on?" It appeared his face was swelling.

It was now hard to understand him. His words were slurred. "Lerg-lerg, allergic reaction. Can't h-have sh-shellfish. C-c-call 911, then take G-Grey a-way. She'll be sc-scared."

"You want me to call 911?"

"H-hurry!" He reached for her, hands quivering so badly that she started to shake when he touched her.

"What? Talk to me, Connor. Tell me what to do." She'd already pulled her phone out.

"N-need to t-t-ell y-you, th-that... I l-lo..." Connor suddenly collapsed and fell on the floor. His body convulsed.

It was almost impossible to breathe. "Connor, Connor, stay with me." She punched the three digits in the phone. *God, if You really exist, don't take him. Help me.*

People had gathered around, staring. Everyone was watching the drama unfold, but not a soul lifted a finger to help. The voice on the phone drew her back to the present. "9-1-1. What's your emergency?"

"Help. My friend just collapsed."

"Is he breathing?"

Aubrey wiped her arm across her face so she could see clearly. "Yes. He said something about an allergic reaction to shellfish."

"Does he have an epi-pen?"

"I, uh, don't know. Wait! He sent his niece out to the truck for his needle."

"What's your address?"

The slapping of feet caught Aubrey's attention. Grey was puffing as she ran toward her. "Abs, Abs. Here's Uncle Connie's needle." She shoved a small yellow box into Aubrey's free hand.

"Your address, ma'am? Please focus."

Aubrey took in Connor. His body was still shaking. *Please help him.*

"Ma'am. What is your location?"

Sudden calmness displaced the almost mind-gripping fear. Aubrey recited the location and then added. "I've got the medication."

"Read the name off the box."

I believe You exist, okay? Help me save him. "The medicine is... ep, ep-epinephrine injection, USP. Is that good?"

"Yes! Open the box and remove the injector."

Aubrey ripped the flap open with shaking hands. Two yellow and black cylinders fell onto her lap. "Got it!"

"Twist the cap off, raise your hand and slam it into his thigh. Do it as hard as you can and keep it there for ten seconds."

Without a thought, Aubrey jumped out of the wheelchair and landed on the floor next to Connor. Pain exploded in her left leg because she landed awkwardly on her cast, but she ignored it. *Please guide my hands.* Grey was suddenly on the floor on the other side of Connor. "I'm scared, Abs."

"Me, too. Stay back." *I know You're there. Please don't take him.* "Watch out." With an arm stroke that would have made Jack the Ripper proud, Aubrey plunged the device into his leg. "One, two... nine, ten."

She threw the spent epi-pen to the side and reached for her phone. "I gave it to him. What do I do now?"

"EMS is three minutes out. If he regains consciousness, keep him calm."

A vision suddenly filled her heart. Of an empty, lonely life without Connor.

Grey's sobs broke the spell. She reached for the girl and held her tightly. A second image slowly appeared, as if it was on a movie screen. Of Aubrey and Connor walking through a pine forest, snow falling heavy on their shoulders while they pulled a sled full of children behind them. He turned and took her in his arms, lips softly caressing hers. "I love you, Aubrey."

Grey shifted, again interrupting the hallucination. Connor was on the floor before her. His eyes were still closed, but his trembling was less than before. She leaned down and placed her head against his cheek. "Stay with me, Connor, please. I need you. I have all along."

Chapter 15

A red-tailed hawk sat on a high limb of a tall tree, looking out over the fields for prey as they approached Wrightsville. He was so tired. Connor allowed his eyes to roll out of focus. The landscape suddenly gave way. The vast expanse of the Susquehanna River unfolded around them. Like an old friend, the arched Route 462 bridge spanning the mile-wide expanse of water that ran parallel to the interstate welcomed him.

"We'll be home soon."

Connor nodded. "Thanks for dropping everything when I got sick. I'm sorry about the whole ordeal. I'm glad you suggested Mimes and Aubrey take Grey home last night."

Leslie coughed into her elbow. "That's okay. I know you just got jealous of me having a few days off, feet propped on the table, binge watching the Hallmark channel and eating pistachios."

He couldn't help but smile at Leslie's wacky sense of humor. "Sometimes I wonder why the state hasn't committed you yet." Snow flurries lazily danced along the highway, swirling together every time a car passed. "Seriously, thanks for being there for me. You and Mimes. Couldn't ask for a better sister or mom."

Leslie reached for his hand and squeezed it. "That's what family is for. But next time, you've gotta be more careful. With your allergies, you had to know the risk of cross-contamination with the shellfish. Why would you even go to a place like that, especially since your first bout of anaphylactic shock was at a hibachi restaurant?"

"Grey wanted to eat there and I wanted the trip to be memorable."

"Well, I'm sure she won't forget yesterday for a long time. I mean it's not every day you see your only uncle almost die in front of you. And to top it off, Grey told me she got a ride in a police car, sirens blaring while rushing her and Aubrey to the hospital. I hope it doesn't happen too frequently for her... riding in the police car, I mean."

"I ruined it for Grey, didn't I? All I wanted was for her to have a good time, one to take her mind off her troubles. And what do I do? I probably scarred her for life. Almost croaked in front of her."

Leslie wiped her cheek. "But you didn't. And that's because God knew we all need and love you too much. I'm just glad Aubrey was along. For both you and Grey."

"Grey looks up to that woman."

Leslie changed lanes to pass a rig that had pulled onto the road at Columbia and was struggling with the slight grade. "I know. Aubrey's been a godsend, hasn't she?" A few seconds of silence followed. "You do realize she saved your life, don't you?"

"I know." He needed to change the subject. A herd of dairy cows was scattered in a muddy brown pasture. Only a few were standing. "Look. Most of the cows are lying down. Must be gonna rain."

Leslie giggled. "But some of them are standing. How many?"

He couldn't help but smile. This old wives' tale was one of those things they'd teased each other about since they were kids. "Maybe ten percent."

"So that equates to a ninety percent chance of rain today."

"Yep." He scratched his arm.

"Are we still on cows or back to Aubrey?"

"We're back on her. What are we going to do when she leaves? Grey will be heartbroken."

Leslie sighed. "The house will seem so empty. Aubrey was a total stranger when she arrived, but now? I'm closer to her than I ever was with Lisa. I really wish Aubrey was our sister—at least my sister. If she was your sister, that'd be weird." Leslie exhaled loudly. "I've thought this situation through while you were gallivanting around the south, tempting fate." Her voice was now soft. "Seriously, there's only one thing to do, Connor."

"What's that?"

"*You* need to convince her to stay."

"Sure, no problem. And how do I go about that?" His left arm was still irritated from where they'd inserted the IV.

"Please don't think I'm meddling."

He shook his head and laughed softly. "Leslie, you've interfered with my life since the day I was born."

His sister smiled. "Only lovingly."

Connor rolled his eyes. "That's your viewpoint."

The seriousness of her voice drew his attention. "We both believe there's a reason for everything— that there are no coincidences. You were meant to be on that train last year when that maniac attacked Aubrey. I was meant to have Rachel Domitar as my roommate in college. Aubrey and Rachel were meant to be friends. Aubrey was in that accident so she could be in a wheelchair. And she was meant to move in here with us. I was meant to get sick so she could go along, and save your life."

He studied his sister's profile. "Go on."

"I believe God did all of this to fulfill His plan, to bring the two of you together."

He shook his head and gazed out the window. "You have no idea how badly I wish that what you're saying was true. But you're missing a key factor. A big problem."

"Like what?"

"My ex-friend Joseph Royer."

"What about him?"

He scoffed. "Do you mean to tell me that an intelligent woman with your Spidey senses can't see Aubrey's in love with him?"

"So?"

"What? Are you not listening? She is in love, l-o-v-e with him. As in the hot Joseph Lance Royer, medical doctor supreme. How could I ever compete with him... and ever stand any chance of winning Aubrey's heart?"

"First, quit telling yourself he's better than you are. Mimes taught us not to allow negative thoughts the light of day so they won't take hold in our hearts. Then, and you listen to me on this, you need to be the man I know you are. Give Aubrey a reason to fall back in love with you."

He almost choked on his saliva. "Back in love? What's that mean?"

"Before you allowed Marci to screw everything up, Aubrey was already in love with you. Mimes and I both saw it." She laughed, which precipitated a coughing spell. "Your mission, Connor Lapp, if you choose to accept it, is to win Aubrey's heart... again."

"It's not that simple."

"Maybe, but I believe with all my soul that it's God's destiny for you two to be together. He'll help you find a way."

Connor could only stare out the window. "I hope so."

***

Aubrey's fingers were jittery. The last time she'd seen Connor was when the EMTs loaded him in the ambulance and he hadn't looked good. Grey had been almost hysterical at that point. It took everything Aubrey had to keep Connor's niece calm. And those hours sitting in the waiting room? They were the longest of her life. As soon as they arrived at the hospital, Aubrey had phoned Leslie to give her the bad news.

After what seemed to be an eternity, the medical staff finally sought out Aubrey and Grey with an update. She'd said a prayer of thanksgiving when they told her that Connor was recovering and would be fine.

Leslie and Mimes had shown up at the hospital soon afterwards. The three adults agreed it would be best to take Grey back to Lancaster. The poor child had been inconsolable and clung tightly to Aubrey. There was no other choice, but while Aubrey had volunteered to go along to comfort the girl, her heart stayed there with Connor.

Warm and delicious aromas wafted in from the kitchen. Mimes was making fresh apple pie.

Grey was standing at the window when she let out a whoop. "They're here, they're here!" Flinging open the front door, Grey ran out.

Aubrey's mouth was dry and a strange feeling nibbled at her insides. Now that she was honest with herself, she knew what it was. Aubrey quickly wheeled out to greet them.

Connor had barely even opened his door when Grey launched herself at him. The rest of the homecoming scene was a little blurry.

Thank You for bringing him home. Aubrey noticed Connor's gait was unsteady as he climbed the ramp to her. Aubrey couldn't wait any longer. She propelled her wheelchair forward and met him halfway, arms wide open. Connor knelt and drew her into a close hug.

"It's so good to see you." His scent, his presence was almost too much. A happy sob escaped her lips.

"Missed you, too." The warmth of his body was such a comfort. "Thanks, Abs." His hands framed her face and he drew away to look into her eyes. "You're my hero. The doctor told me you saved my life."

She held his face in her hands. The depth of those big blue eyes drew her in. "I'd never been more worried in my life." *I almost lost you.* "I had no clue what to do, but between Grey bringing your medicine and the 911 operator talking me through it... you made it."

The corners of his mouth curled slightly. "They told me you were the one who gave me the epi-pen, is that right?"

"Yes. I hope I did it okay."

He winked and rubbed his leg. "So that explains the ginormous bruise on my leg?"

Her face warmed. "I'm sorry. That was the first time I ever did that."

"And hopefully the last, at least to me."

Despite the glow of his face, she could sense his exhaustion. "How about we go inside? Maybe we could watch a movie or something."

He nodded. "That would be the second best thing about today."

"So, if relaxing with a movie is second best, what's first?"

To Aubrey's surprise, he hugged her again. Her heart skipped a beat when his lips brushed her hair. "The best thing was coming home... and seeing you. Definitely the highpoint of my day."

Leslie's laugh interrupted the euphoria of seeing Connor. "Why don't we head inside? Grey told me Mimes has hot apple pie and vanilla ice cream waiting."

Connor answered his sister, but his eyes were on Aubrey. "Sounds like that's exactly what I need."

"I agree." Leslie turned Aubrey's chair around and pushed. Connor's hand touched her arm. Without thinking, she slowly intertwined her fingers with his. *This is exactly where I belong.*

The wondrous bouquet of baked apple pie mingled with the cinnamon and brown sugar crumb topping. Each steaming slice was cooled by the creamy vanilla ice cream that puddled around the crust. But Aubrey didn't really notice the food. Her attention was focused on the hand still holding hers.

Mimes interrupted Aubrey's growing fantasy. "I'd like to give the blessing today." Little fingers grabbed Aubrey's other hand as everyone joined hands. "Lord, we thank You for this bounty and also for our many blessings." Her voice rose an octave. "And thank You for bringing my son home."

Grey went next. "Thanks, God, for my Uncle Connie being safe."

Leslie followed. "Thank you for my brother, and for Aubrey being there to save him. And I know this is a big request, but can You give Connor the wisdom to make better choices? When he's about to falter, please remind him how much we need him. Amen."

Aubrey had to swallow her giggle when Connor cleared his throat. "Not so fast, Leslie. Father above, I want to thank You for blessing me with the love that surrounds me." The tone of his voice changed. It was now somber, almost reverent. "And thanks for giving me another chance. Guide my life. Show me the reason You let me live. Amen."

The grip on her left hand relaxed, but Aubrey tightened hers. "May I add to the blessing?" A quick scan around the table revealed various looks of surprise.

Mimes smiled at her. "Please go ahead, Aubrey."

Aubrey's mouth was suddenly dry. *We made a deal.* Her eyes gravitated to the sign above the stairs—the one that started, 'As for me and my house...' A quick hand hug from Connor made her smile. "Uh, God? I'm kind of new at this, but I wanted to thank You for helping Connor pull through last night. When You sent me here, I guess I was kind of lost. But living here has taught me about... love and family. Thank You for this, this... for *my* family. Uh, amen."

Total silence surrounded her. Aubrey lifted her head. All eyes were opened wide. Connor squeezed her hand again. The look of wonder awaited her. A voice whispered in her ear. *"This is the home I've prepared for you."*

Connor's smile was ear to ear. "Amen."

Chapter 16

Joe Rohrer stepped from the room and dropped his patient's chart in the basket. He had just turned toward the next examination room when a hand touched his shoulder. He spun to see the smiling face of the office manager, his friend Daisy Elliot.

"Dr. Rohrer, you have a call waiting for you." The corners of her lips were twitching. *She's up to something.* "Thought you might want to take it before you see your next patient."

Two can play at this. "Hmm. It's rare that I get interrupted between patients, except for emergencies. Is this a crisis?"

He could easily tell she was teasing him. "I don't know."

"Do you know who the call is from?"

"Um-hmm." Her eyes were full of merriment.

"Okay, spill the beans, Daze. Who is it?"

Daisy winked at him. "Your Aubrey."

He felt his cheeks warm. *My Aubrey? Yes!* "So do you know what she wants?"

The girl giggled and gave him a parting shot. "I believe I do, Dr. Rohrer, I believe I do. She's waiting for you on line two."

His nurse appeared. "Dr. Rohrer, Mr. Kline is waiting for you in exam three."

"Would you please tell the patient I'll be with him shortly?" Joe slipped into his office and closed the door. *Breathe normal.* He picked up the receiver and depressed the button. "Hello?"

"Uh, hi Joe. It's Aubrey. This a bad time?"

"No, of course not. I'm seeing patients, but I can spare a few minutes. Let me guess. You were wondering where I'm taking you for dinner tonight, right?"

A long pause. "About that. I can't make our date this evening."

A shiver ran down his arm. "Is everything okay?"

"Not really. I, uh, I don't quite know how to say this..."

"You know you can say anything you want." A nasty thought entered his mind. Did this call have to do with the rat who'd had her to himself for the weekend? "Wait, are you canceling because of Connor?"

"Yes."

"Really? What did the little backstabber do?"

"It's not like that. Connor, well, he almost passed away this weekend."

Joe's mouth went dry. "Connor almost died? What happened?"

"He had a severe food reaction."

Joe felt guilt rising in his stomach. "Anaphylaxis. How is he now?"

"Connor's okay, well maybe a little weak."

"Good thing he has his sister and mother there to take care of him. So, why are you breaking our date?"

"Joe," again a very long silence. "I almost lost him. I was so scared he was dying and I uh... well, I realized how much I care for Connor. I have all along."

Joe felt like a rogue wave slammed into his body, leaving him wet and fighting for breath on the hard, wet sand. The exact feelings he'd felt when Tara had phoned him to say she'd decided to stay with Edmund. "I thought you liked *me*."

"I do, I really do. It's just..."

Everything in the room now took on a red tinge. "You know, Aubrey, I never would have dreamed you were the kind of girl who would dump me over the phone. Guess I really *overestimated* how classy you are."

"Joe, it's not like that. I just... Can we still be friends?"

"Yeah, sure. I need to get back to my patients. Wait. Who's taking you to get your casts off? Me or... *him*?"

"Would you be upset if Connor took me?"

His anger was about to boil over. "I really don't care. Goodbye, Ms. Stettinger." He slammed the receiver down. Joe's eye caught the photo sitting on his desk, the one of Aubrey from their date on the Strasburg Railroad. Ripping it off the desk, he threw it against the wall where it pinwheeled into the floor lamp. The luminaire crashed to the tile, shards of glass flying everywhere.

An immediate banging shook the door. "Dr. Rohrer, are you okay in there?" Daisy's voice flowed to him.

"I'm fine."

"Can I come in?"

Damn you, Connor. He was shaking his head. "I don't care."

The door flew open. Several of the office staff were gathered outside, obviously trying to find out what was going on. *Busybodies.*

Daisy quickly entered, firmly shutting it to keep out prying eyes. "Joe, what happened?"

He pointed his finger at the phone and acted as if he was pulling the trigger to shoot the device. "Can you believe Aubrey just dumped me?"

"No. What happened?"

Joe ran his fingers through his hair. "She called me to say Connor had a severe food reaction and almost died, and he's so helpless and she realizes she cares for him and yada, yada, yada."

Daisy touched his hand. "I'm so sorry. What can I do?"

"Tell me the truth. What's wrong with me? First, Tara leaves me and goes back to that slime ball Edmund. She ended up marrying him. Then Aubrey tosses me to the side like a piece of scrap paper just because of Connor."

A headache was quickly overtaking him. *Get control of yourself.* His voice was calmer. "What's so despicable about me, Daisy? I try to be kind and respectful. I never push, never demand my own way. Am I that revolting that no one wants me?"

Daisy's blue eyes were subdued. "There's absolutely nothing wrong with you, Joe. Any girl would be lucky to have you."

"Sure. How did Aubrey put it? We can still be friends."

"The timing just hasn't been right yet. But one of these days, you'll look up and there she'll be, the woman of your dreams. Be patient. It's all in God's time, not ours."

"Easy for you to say. You found your Mr. Right."

"Yes, I did. But did I ever tell you the whole story?"

His eyes met her face.

Despite the smile, there was a sadness there. "I fell in love with Jake the minute I met him. I was thirteen and I instantly knew I'd just been introduced to the man God intended for me. But the timing wasn't right and Jake didn't even seem to know I existed. He married Callie when I was fourteen and my heart was broken. Then two years ago, right in this office, Jake came back into my life. I was thirty-one. Eighteen years after I first fell in love with him."

A stray tear dribbled from her left eye. "I forgot. Thanks for the words of hope, Daisy."

She walked around the desk and hugged him. "Have faith, Joe. I truly believe God has someone really special planned for you."

Such a good friend. "I hope you're right."

***

Aubrey smiled at the man who was driving. *So handsome.* "Thanks for taking me to get my casts off."

173

"My pleasure. Can you believe you've been here over three months?"

"No way. It only seems like a few days. Time passes differently here in the country."

"That's for sure. What's the first thing you're going to do when you're back on your feet?"

"Hmm, let me see..." Her hand was against her chin. "Maybe a long walk or dancing or, ooh, ooh... I know. A long, hot bath."

His expression darkened. "Finally free. Bet you can't wait to head back to the big city, huh?"

I don't want to go back anymore. "I was thinking about what you said."

When she looked in his direction, his eyebrows were raised. "I've said an awful lot. Can you be more specific?"

Read between the lines. "When you were talking about all Grey is going through. You know, because her mom's moving away and not taking Grey with her. And both you and Leslie said she kind of likes me."

He smiled at her. "If that's all you heard, we need to work on your active listening skills. Grey both loves and adores you, Aubrey."

"So she's said. I love her, too. Grey's a very special child. She reminds me of... well, me, you know, when I was a kid. I remember the loneliness, and how tough it was. I just don't want her to go through the same things I did."

"So how does this relate to whatever I said?"

Here goes. "Well, I was thinking... maybe I could delay leaving for a while, you know, to be here for her. Do you think Leslie would mind if I stayed for a while longer?" *Until we see where you and I are going.*

The smile lighting his face grew. "That would make her day." Connor reached across the seat and took her hand. "I would love that, too."

Really? "Thank you." He was silent for a moment. "Everything okay?"

"I wasn't going to mention anything, but maybe I should tell you now. I had a dream about you last night."

Her arms began to tingle and her chest warmed. "A dream? About me?"

"Yeah. You were a little girl, splashing in the creek, wearing big red boots. I was fishing, but wasn't catching anything... because of you. So, I walked over and asked you not to scare the fish away."

Did I tell him about my big red galoshes? "Did I quit?"

"We both stopped what we were doing. You took my hand and led me on this hike through a forest to the top of a mountain. By then, the sun was setting on a valley. There was a lake, surrounded by the greenest trees I'd ever seen. It was absolutely beautiful."

She waited for him to continue, but he stopped. "Is that all?"

He squeezed her hand. "No. We sat and talked, watching the stars replace the setting sun. Then, when I turned to you..."

Tell me you kissed me. "What happened next?"

"You were older, same age as now. But..."

His eyes had a dreamy look. "Yes?"

175

He blushed. "I, uh, you could say it was like a vision inside the dream and it hit me as kind of odd."

"What did?"

He pulled into the doctor's lot, found a space and shifted into park. Connor turned to face her. His blue eyes were soft and so enchanting. "I never dream in color. I think that was the first time. And know what, Aubrey?"

A warm feeling crawled into her thoughts. For whatever reason, she knew this moment was significant. She couldn't wait for him to speak, yet she didn't want to rush the feeling. His hands brushed the hair back from her eyes. His face drew closer. "Yes?"

"The dream, it felt so real and... perfect. Especially the last part."

Aubrey studied him intently. Her whole body was tingling. "Don't keep me in suspense. What was it?"

The depth of his eyes tugged her in deeper. "You and I were much older. We were on another road trip, with Grey. And even she was older, maybe late teens or early twenties. But something magical had occurred."

"And what was that."

Connor's blushing face was now blood red. "We'd become a real family, just the three of us."

***

Despite it being a Tuesday afternoon, the lot was full. The wind had picked up, leaves racing with each other as the wind swirled across the lot. Connor opened the truck door and offered his arm. Aubrey took it so she could balance herself. She stumbled slightly, but he caught her. "You okay, ace?"

She nodded, and behind those brown eyes, he could see joy. "First day on new legs. It'll come back."

"Would it be better with the chair?"

She quickly shook her head. "I prefer not to use it. Like the doc said, a little at a time."

Connor swung the door open and they walked in. The owner, Sophie Miller, was talking to a pretty black-haired woman. The other lady smiled, revealing two dimples—one on her chin and the other on her right cheek. Sophie greeted the couple. "Welcome back to Essence of Tuscany. Are you here for afternoon tea?"

"Yes, please. Aubrey and I are celebrating the end of her casts."

Ms. Miller slowly led them to a table along the window. "Well, congratulations. When I was in my teens, I had a broken leg. It was in the summertime and oh so annoying. I was incredibly glad when I was able to get rid of that cast. Here's your table." She hovered until Aubrey was seated. "To celebrate your new freedom, I'll send out a special treat, on the house."

The smile on Aubrey's face was like the dawn of a new day. "Boy, you look so happy."

She giggled and touched his hand. "I always took being able to walk for granted."

"Well, you got it back. How would you like to spend the rest of the day?"

She wrinkled her nose at him. "This is going to sound corny, but can we go to that market you and

Leslie talk about? Was it Roots Auction?" Connor nodded. "I think I'd like to cook dinner tomorrow, as a thank you. I'll pick up some fresh veggies. And then maybe we could find a bookstore? I want to get a few books for Grey."

You're amazing. "So you get your freedom back and the first thing you want to do is take care of others?"

"Is that okay?"

"Absolutely."

"Hi, guys." They both looked up at the petite blonde with thick hair. She smiled, and then placed two mini pies topped with whipped cream in front of them. "These are apple-raspberry crumb delights. Compliments of Sophie. I'm Ashley and I'll be taking care of you today. What can I get for you?"

After they ordered, Connor's hand accidentally brushed against Aubrey's. Her fingers wrapped around his. "So you were telling me about the things you want to do."

Her eyes now gleamed. "I want to live. Now don't think I'm not grateful to you and Leslie for taking me into your beautiful home, but being cramped up wasn't quite my style."

"Well then, let's come up with a plan. What would Aubrey like to do?"

"I saw there's a theater in town."

He'd never seen her this happy. *You glow, Abs.* "Hey, Lancaster is a cultural metropolis. We've got four. There's Rainbow Dinner Theater, Dutch Apple, Sight and Sound and American Music Theater. Which one were you thinking about?"

"Um, maybe all of them, in time. *Oklahoma* is playing at Dutch Apple. The five of us could go. Has Grey ever been to the theater?"

"Not that I'm aware of. Wait, you said the five of us?"

"Yes, you and me, Grey, Leslie and Mimes. You know, the whole family."

Is this happening? Before he could answer, Ashley delivered two pots of tea. When the girl walked away, Connor couldn't help but notice the happy expression on the curly-haired girl's face. "Can I ask a personal question?"

She smiled as she poured cream into her tea. "Of course."

"What happened?"

Her eyes were open wider, but that smile was growing. "When?"

"Over the last week. Not that I'm complaining, but it's like it's a whole new you. You seem so, so... ecstatic and..." he squeezed her hand. "There seems to be something magical going on between us. Have you noticed it?" *Did I really just say that?*

"Connor, I owe you a gigantic apology."

What? "I don't understand."

She traced her index finger across the back of his hand. "Coming here has been completely different from anything I've ever experienced."

"Good, I hope."

Aubrey nodded as she pulled her hand back, but her eyes were focused on her teacup. "There's so much about my past you don't know."

"You don't need to tell me. We all have pasts."

"Somehow, I doubt you do."

Maybe someday I'll have the courage to tell you. "I appreciate you saying that..."

"Let's just say I have serious trust issues. Remember the first day I moved here?"

He laughed. "Oh, the day when you accused me of setting it all up?"

The teacup must have been extremely interesting, but the corners of her mouth turned up slightly. "Yeah, a great example of how not to make friends and influence people."

"Well, you do have a point. And now I owe you an apology."

Her eyes finally met his. "You do? Why?"

"I judged you that day, and... I was wrong."

"We're past that. Please let me finish."

"Sorry."

Aubrey took a sip of her tea. "When you gave Marci a second chance, I thought you were playing games with me. But after I witnessed your actions in the last couple of days and the things you did for Grey, I think I understand you better now. You almost died because you put Grey first. And that was because you were trying to be kind to her, wasn't it?"

"Maybe, but about Marci? Stupid is what that was."

She nodded. "I'd prefer to believe it's your kindness." Connor noted her hands were shaking. "Can I ask you a question? And... and I need you to be painfully honest with me."

Her words struck a nerve, but the look in her eyes warmed him. "Ask me anything."

Her cheeks colored, brightly. "That day, on the train, did you feel, uh, what did you think..."

Connor answered before she could finish. "I was very attracted to you. Leaving you standing there at the station when I left was the hardest thing I ever did in my life."

"Why?"

Now Connor could feel his face heating. "I'm not sure. Did you ever have a moment in time when you knew everything in your life had changed?"

She nodded, eyes wide open. "That's exactly how I felt that day."

Connor reached across the table. Aubrey met him halfway. "You did?"

She smiled. "Yes. Can you do me a favor?"

"Of course."

"I feel bad for rushing off to date someone else. Can you give me a second chance, just like you did Marci?"

Chapter 17

"**A**re you sure you're gonna be warm enough in that outfit?" Connor stood, looking at his niece. Dressed as Moana, Grey was sporting one of the fresh white Hawaiian plumeria leis around her neck that Aubrey had ordered. Grey nodded and smiled as she munched on her brownie. Tonight was the annual Lapp Halloween party, the envy of the community. The massive bank barn was decked for the celebration.

"I think Moana will be fine, but she better watch how much sugar she eats." The touch of Aubrey's skin was warm as she wound her arm through his. She looked absolutely gorgeous tonight, decked out as Sina, Moana's mother. And Connor's costume? He was dressed as Chief Tui, Moana's father *and* Sina's husband! Grey had begged for them to dress like this and of course, Aubrey made Grey's wishes come true.

"The guests are beginning to arrive." Connor turned to find his sister standing there. Leslie was dressed as Tala, Moana's grandmother. She smiled. "We do look like a happy family, don't we?"

Connor couldn't resist. "Yep. And did you notice how we're all dressed exactly like our personalities? Grey as the smart, sweet heroine. Aubrey as the wise and beautiful island queen. Me as the handsome village chieftain. And Leslie, as the crazy old lady. Just perfect."

Leslie jabbed him in the ribs. "Village chieftain? I thought you were the village idiot."

Grey laughed. *So glad to see her happy.* "Next year me and Aubrey are going to dress like Anna and Elsa, aren't we, Abs?" *Frozen* was Grey's second favorite Disney movie.

Aubrey squeezed Connor's hand. "Absolutely. And should we get Uncle Connie to dress like Kristoff?"

Leslie chimed in. "I think he'd be better off cast as Sven, the smelly reindeer." Connor's sister turned to her niece. "Come help me greet the guests."

Connor took a parting shot at his sibling. "See ya, Grandma."

Leslie returned the volley. "Later, Paw Tui!"

Aubrey turned to face him, her hands so warm in his. And the sparkle in her eyes? Dazzling. "So, my chieftain, what would you like to do?"

Kiss you? Their lips hadn't yet met, but he'd been dreaming about it. "Spending time with you suits me fine." He touched her cheek. "What you just said to Grey, did you mean it?"

"What do you mean?"

"About being here, for next Halloween?"

"I'm hoping so, but maybe Grey will get tired of me." He could see the joviality in her eyes.

"You know better than that."

She winked. "Then maybe I'll wear out my welcome."

"Never. At least not before all the stars burn out." He leaned toward her, close to those plump and beautiful lips. Aubrey tilted her head and closed her eyes. Her hand was against his cheek, pulling him close.

Connor's eyes drifted shut, in anticipation of heaven. A loud voice spoiled the moment. "Connor, Connor Lapp? Is that really you?"

Aubrey released him. He turned to find a woman he didn't immediately recognize. With the mask on, he didn't have a clue who she was.

"Yes, I'm Connor Lapp... and you are?"

She lifted her mask and his mouth was suddenly desert dry. "Chrissy Berryman. Remember me?"

Connor knew her, but wished he didn't. "Uh, how are you?" He was fumbling for something to say.

"I know you." Connor almost jumped at Aubrey's voice. Again, she threaded her arm through his. There was something in her tone that caught his attention. "You delivered flowers here a couple weeks back."

"Wow. I almost didn't recognize you. Wait, weren't you in a wheelchair then?"

"You have a good memory."

"Yes, I do. Your name's Abigail, right?"

Connor noted the look on Aubrey's face—something he hadn't seen before. *Defiance or maybe possessiveness?* "Close. I'm Aubrey, Aubrey Stettinger."

Chrissy's eyes narrowed, as did her pitch. "That's right. How could I forget? Aubrey Stettinger. Someone told me you were only staying here until you recovered. And now look at you, walking with the big boys and girls now, huh? I was told you were heading back to the Big Apple."

Aubrey entwined her fingers in Connor's hand. "Is that a fact?"

Chrissy's smile left. "If you're recovered, why are you still in Paradise? Will you be leaving soon?"

Aubrey fluffed up her hair as if to show she didn't really care. "That depends."

"Really? On what?"

"On what Connor and I decide."

Ms. Berryman crossed her arms and shuffled her eyes between the two of them. "About what?"

Good question. What are we deciding? Connor felt like he was watching a tennis match and now the ball was in Aubrey's side of the court.

Aubrey's grip on his hand was cutting off his circulation. "Our future, you know? What we're going to do. I thought perhaps our matching costumes would have given you a hint. You see, we're very, *very* close friends and we really enjoy each other's company. Now, if you'll excuse us, we have festivities to attend to. Nice seeing you again." Aubrey spun away, pulling Connor along.

He whispered, "What was that about?"

Aubrey stopped in her tracks and turned Connor to face her. "Our party's been crashed."

"What?"

"I saw how pale your face turned when you recognized Chrissy. I don't think you invited her. I certainly didn't and I'm pretty sure Leslie didn't either. And then there's the other thing."

"I'm not following you."

"The person she walked in with. I didn't recognize the other woman until she ran her fingers through her hair."

"Who was it?"

"Pure trouble. About six foot tall. Short red hair. Smug, better-than-everyone smile."

Connor's eyes widened. "Marci's here?"

"Don't look now, but she's right behind you."

***

Connor whipped around to face his ex. Aubrey watched his face turn red.

Marci was sporting a sweet smile. "Well hello, Connor." She swiveled her gaze and nodded. "Nice to see you again, Aubrey. I see you're standing on your own, so congratulations on your recovery."

"What are you doing here?" Connor fumed.

"I just came to the party. Leslie does such a great job decorating."

"You weren't invited."

Marci reached out to touch his face. "Yes, I was."

He shook his head to get her off him. "By whom? I'm pretty sure neither Leslie nor Aubrey gave you an invitation."

Marci placed both hands on her cheeks and fawned surprise. "Don't you remember?"

"Exactly what am I supposed to remember?"

"Oh my. I can't believe you forgot. Why Connor, you were the one who invited me."

Chills were running down Aubrey's arms. *Connor invited Marci?*

"And when did I supposedly invite you?"

Marci swept her hand through that short, red hair again. "Why, last year. Don't you remember? It was here, in this exact place. You had just kissed me, and told me how you would love me forever. Then you said we'd wear matching costumes this year."

Connor trembled. "That was before we broke up."

She flicked her hand at him, as if she were swatting a fly. "We didn't break up. We just had a spat." The red-haired woman reached forward and took his hand. "I've missed you, Connor, especially your sweet kisses and the way your touch excites me at night."

Connor ripped his hand away. "Enough. Get out of here."

Marci tilted her head and smiled. "Or what, baby? Will you forcibly throw me out, or perhaps call the authorities? That would make quite a fuss."

His words came out between clenched teeth. "If I need to. Please leave, now, before you make a scene."

Marci laughed and turned her attention to Aubrey. "You need to watch him, Aubrey. He has quite a temper. And there's something you should know about the Lapps. They're painfully mindful of their public image. I mean, just consider how they quietly covered up Grey's parents' divorce, and all the nasty things that happened between that couple. I'm sure they kept it from you."

A great storyteller. Easy to see why you're a writer. Aubrey had to give it to her, Marci's words were perfectly crafted. Still, Aubrey stood up to her.

"I know everything I need to know about this family."

Marci's eyes widened and her smile ignited. "Really? Do you know about Connor's past, and what kind of a man he was before he met me?"

Connor pulled away from Aubrey. He was pointing at the door. His voice was high pitched. "Get out of here, *now*."

The tall woman touched his face. "Or what, sweetie?"

Connor slapped her hand away. "Leave, now."

Marci winked at Aubrey. "And watch out for his temper." Her attention moved back to Connor. "If that's what you want, Connor. We'll pick this up later." She started to turn away, but then pivoted back toward them. Aubrey, specifically. "A word of advice to you. Connor isn't what he seems to be." Marci's eyes momentarily took in Connor before shuffling back to Aubrey. "In case you didn't find out yet, Connor has a dark, cruel side, a selfish side. He likes to take things, especially from innocent, unsuspecting women. Things they regret losing, and can never replace."

Aubrey shook her head. "I see right through you. You're evil, Marci. Why don't you pretend to be a human with some shred of decency, and go?"

Marci's laugh was unexpected. She placed her hand against Aubrey's cheek. "Oh my sweet, innocent child. He has you under his spell, doesn't he?"

Aubrey shoved Marci away. "Get out of here and away from *my* family."

Again, Marci feigned kindness. "Ah, poor Aubrey. He hasn't done it to you, yet. If I were you, I'd run.

He'll just hurt you, after he plays his games and takes what you can't get back. Don't believe me? Ask Chrissy Berryman what he did to her." Marci's eyes narrowed. "How he ruined her life, destroyed her happiness and left her suffering all alone after he got what he wanted. That's who Connor really is."

"Marci, what in God's name are you doing here?" Aubrey turned to the source of the angry voice. Leslie.

"Hi, Les."

"I told you never to call me that, didn't I? Get off my property, now."

Marci's smile was again sweet. "Of course, Les. I don't want to upset you." Marci held her hand to her mouth as if she were telling Aubrey a secret. "Her manly side, you know? Another Lapp family secret. This house is full of them. Well, it was nice to see you again, Aubrey. *Bon voyage*. And Connor? Call me. I'll let you pick up where you left off."

Leslie extracted a phone from somewhere under her costume. "That's it. I'm calling the police."

Marci again laughed, but this time it wasn't jovial, but almost villainous. "No need. I was just leaving. Ta-ta everyone." Marci strode away, collecting Chrissy as they exited.

Leslie's eyes grew large and she turned to face her brother. "Was that Chris Berryman?"

Connor's jaws were clamped together. "Um-hmm."

"Why was she here? I thought you had a restraining order against her."

A what? Connor turned to face Leslie. "Yeah, I do."

***

Aubrey's touch was light against his arm. "A restraining order?"

"It's a long story." He could see disappointment growing in Aubrey's eyes. *I've no choice but to tell her. The whole truth.* He quickly turned to Leslie. "Aubrey and I will be back in a few minutes. I think we both need some fresh air."

Leslie eyed him warily. "You okay?"

"I think so."

"Good, you two talk. I'll tend to the guests." Leslie turned back to the party.

Connor offered his hand to Aubrey. She stared at it for a second before taking it. He could feel her shudder at his touch.

Outside, he turned to her. In the darkness, he saw Aubrey shake her head. "Let's go someplace where I can see your face clearly."

"The porch?"

"No. I want to sit across from you. How about inside?"

"Okay." The silence between them filled him with dread. *We've come so far...* After entering the house, he followed her to the table and, as she requested, they sat face to face from each other.

"What just happened?"

"Marci just wanted to stir up trouble with her baseless lies."

Aubrey cocked her head. "It's taken me a long time to allow myself to trust you like I do. I have high hopes for us. I know she has an agenda, but explain what she meant." She squeezed his hand. "And please, no secrets. I need to know everything."

None from you. He nodded. "Long before you met me, I was a different man. Er, well not really a man, but something much less. I was full of pride, full of self-assurance. I only cared about Connor Lapp. I did a lot of things I'm ashamed of now."

Her voice was soft. "That's not who you are today. Is it?"

It was hard to meet her eyes, but he did. "Hope not. I believed I could have anything I wanted. Nothing was off limits. And, well, sometimes I took those things without caring about who it hurt."

"Are you talking about Chrissy?"

"Yes. She was a year behind me in high school. I never paid much attention to her, but I knew she had a big crush on me. I couldn't have cared less. She always hung around with the same loser, a guy named Aaron Peck. Aaron and I were very different. I was outgoing, he was shy. Me, an athlete. Him, a nerd. I knew I was handsome and all that. He certainly wasn't."

Laughter from outside caught his attention. "In between my sophomore and junior years at college, I ran into them at the pool. Chrissy was very... well, very attractive in her swimsuit and I couldn't stop staring at her. Even after I noticed the engagement ring on her hand, I ogled her so much that Aaron noticed. Words were said and, well, it turned into a shoving match. We ended up in the parking lot. Several of my friends tagged along. They were there to watch me win, to teach this dud a lesson. Thought I knew how to fight, but Aaron beat the crap out of me. Seems the little nerd had earned himself a black belt in karate."

Connor shook his head and stared at his hands. Aubrey's fingers gripped his. "Go on."

"I decided to get back at Aaron. It felt like a game, some competition. I may have fallen behind in the first quarter, but I came up with a plan. I was scared to duke it out with Aaron again, so I decided to hurt him in another way. I went after Chrissy."

"Oh, Connor. You didn't, did you?"

"Afraid I did. And she fell for it, hard. Within a month, I'd not only driven a wedge between them, I forced them apart. She broke off her engagement to Aaron. Led her to believe I wanted her as my wife."

"Is that what you told her?"

He raised his eyes to hers. Those deep brown eyes were watchful, but not as condemning as he expected. "Yes. I lied to her. I had no intention of ever putting a ring on her finger. It was all about hurting Aaron. I never had any real feelings for Chrissy."

"That was horribly wrong, but I don't believe that's news to you."

"I know. After she broke it off with Aaron, he enlisted in the Navy and left Lancaster. But Chrissy, she was ready to start a life together. With me. In the fall, when college started back up, I tried to quit seeing her."

"What do you mean, tried?"

"As in, I tried. She refused to let go. Chrissy started showing up when I had classes, when I went to church. I lived at home with my parents in those days. The crazy girl was stalking me. I warned her it was over, but she wouldn't listen." *Wish I could undo the past.*

193

"Is that why you had to get a restraining order?"

"No. Not until Chrissy started breaking into the house. I'd wake up and find her in bed with me. And every time I'd tell her to leave, she'd beg me to marry her. The girl refused to leave me alone. I had no choice."

Aubrey rubbed his arm. "She couldn't let go."

"Nope. I screwed up royally. I never meant to hurt her, but I did."

Aubrey sighed. "She delivered flowers here to the house, a while back. And she asked about you. There was something in her eyes that day. I could tell she had loved you."

"I think she did. But it wasn't reciprocated, at all. All I did was hurt that poor girl and destroy her future. I caused her to break off the engagement with Aaron. Ruined it for both of them."

"And is that what Marci meant by you taking something from Chrissy she can't get back?"

"Yes."

"Marci insinuated Chrissy wasn't the only one. Is that true?"

Where do I begin? "I did a lot of bad things when I was younger. Regrets I'll carry to the grave." He sought out her eyes. "But what I did to Chrissy, it's, it's..."

"Unforgivable?"

"I tried to turn over a new leaf. Wanted to be a man I could be proud of when I look back at the end of my life. Perhaps that's why I overcompensated with Marci."

Aubrey laughed. *That's odd.* "What's so funny?"

"God has a sense of humor."

"Huh?"

She placed her hands over his. "He paid you back. I believe you met your match."

"I don't understand."

"Marci acts just like you used to, or as you described. Connor, she never loved you. It was all a game to her."

Never thought of it that way. She stood and Connor matched her actions. "Can you forgive me?"

"There's absolutely nothing you did to me."

"I mean about my past."

There was merriment in her eyes. "I appreciate your honesty. You don't understand how important that is to me." She traced a heart on the palm of his hand. Her smile was dazzling. "The past is the past and by now you should know it's not your past I'm interested in, Connor Lapp."

For whatever reason, his heart lifted and he felt playful. He turned Aubrey so she fully faced him. "Really? Then what might it be? My good looks? My charm?"

Her hand was on the back of his neck. Those moist, plump lips were only millimeters away from his. Aubrey's voice was as soft as a baby's sigh. "Not even close. What if we think about what our future holds?" The warmth in those brown pools of bliss were pure delight. "I think it's high time you kissed me, Connor."

Chapter 18

D espite the date on the calendar, it was warm this morning. Aubrey and Rachel were taking a walk along the road where the Lapps lived. The red painted barn on the Stolztfus dairy farm loomed before them. Aubrey chuckled to herself as Rachel fanned the air. "What in heaven's name is that odor?"

It was quite pungent this morning. "The smell of Lancaster County money. To amateurs like you and me, the smell is cow manure, but more specifically, dairy cow poop. The black and white ones are called Holsteins. You'll have to get used to the smell if you plan on visiting me in the future."

She could feel Rachel's gaze. "Future? You're really going to stay here in Lancaster?"

"Um-hmm."

"I don't get it. Three weeks ago, you were chomping at the bit to move back to the Big Apple. What changed your mind, sexy Joe Rohrer?"

Aubrey couldn't help but smile. "Nope, Mr. Wonderful, Connor Lapp."

Rachel's mouth fell open. "I thought the whole ordeal between Connor and his ex-girlfriend drove a wedge between the two of you. And the last thing I heard, you and the good doctor were about to get hot and heavy. You have got to do a better job keeping me in the loop, girl."

A buggy was approaching from behind them. Aubrey waited until it passed. "Did I tell you what's happening with Grey?"

"I'm having trouble following this. What does that little girl have to do with anything?"

"Her mom suddenly remarried and moved to California. She left Grey here to finish school. And her worthless dad, he ignores the poor child."

"What? You're all over the place, girl. Now you're staying because of the child?"

"Not really. Leslie and Connor planned to take her away for a weekend to cheer her up, but Leslie got sick, so Grey asked me to go in her place."

Rachel stopped. "Wait. You went away for a weekend with Connor?"

Aubrey was smiling ear to ear. "Connor and Grey."

"And what happened?"

She reached for her friend's hands. "My eyes were opened. I got to see first-hand Connor's compassion and respect. And it all became quite clear."

"I'm not following you."

"The deal with Marci wasn't affection. He felt sorry for her."

"Aubrey, this isn't making sense."

"I was struggling with it, too. But then when he almost died—"

"Huh? Almost died? This sounds like a soap opera." The scent from the barn was almost overwhelming. "Man, does that stink. We'll name it *The Young and the Breathless*."

Aubrey frowned as she remembered the nightmare. "It does sound like it's made up, doesn't it? Anyway, Connor had a horrible reaction to seafood and went into anaphylactic shock. It was so scary. At the hospital, two visions came to me."

"Visions?"

"God let me see how my life would be without Connor in it, and then, what my remaining days would be like with him. How wonderful my future might be."

Rachel shook her head in disbelief. "God showed you? Wow, there must be something in the water here. Imagine Aubrey Stettinger talking about God like He's real?"

Aubrey could feel her face warm. "I'm convinced now. But the point I'm trying to make is my eyes were opened. I realized I want to spend my life with Connor, and inside, I know he feels the same way. And this family... I want to be part of it. Rachel, Leslie offered me a fulltime job, which I accepted. Decided I'm not going back to New York."

"What about your dream of getting on Broadway?"

Sadness crept into her heart. "Dreams change. I'll be thirty in a few years. There's no guarantee I'd ever get there."

"But before this happened, you had made it. Your dream was within your reach. Are you ready to let that go?"

"Part of me still wants that, but Rach, I feel like my place, my future is here. Dreams sometimes evolve and... maybe become even sweeter."

"Wow. This is surreal. It's like you're a completely different woman. Maybe I should move to Paradise."

"That would be so cool. You'd love it here. Would you really consider relocating?"

"Fill me in on you and Connor."

Her body warmed at the thought of him. "We're seeing where it's going, and I'm thinking it's heading someplace good, really, *really* good."

"Like..."

"Like, I, uh, trust him, totally. And for the first time in my life, I think I've fallen in love."

Rachel laughed. "How did all this happen?"

"With God's nudge... And the help of a madman. The one He placed on that train."

***

The salty tang of the melted butter mixed with the bitterness of the fresh chopped onions. "You do realize how lucky you are, having such a handsome and devoted brother playing sous chef, don't you?" He poured the thick yellow liquid over the chopped bread. Connor and Leslie were making filling balls for the Thanksgiving meal.

Leslie teased back. "Having a wonderful, intelligent and benevolent sister who employs you, provides room and board and guides you every step of the way through your life should be what you're thankful for." She was mixing the filling with her bare hands. "Can you pour some milk in here? Just a little—whoa. Perfect."

Connor's heart was happy. His words were somber. "I'm very blessed. Leslie, in all seriousness, I hope you know how much I appreciate... well, everything. Especially our closeness. And for helping me be the man I've become. For your guidance with Aubrey. Words could never express how glad I am that you're my sister."

She turned, eyes now glistening. "I feel the same way. From the moment you saved me when I fell overboard... and through everything that's happened since. I appreciate you, too." She gave Connor a tight hug before releasing him and returning to her food preparation.

Connor pulled off a couple of sheets of aluminum foil and reached for the aerosolized olive oil. "Are these big enough?"

"Yes, but don't use that. Take a stick of butter and coat the foil."

"That takes longer. Why are you giving me busy work?"

She shook her head, but there was a smile on her lips. "The filling gets browner when you use butter. But I should have expected it. You always try to take the easy way out, don't you?"

"What are you saying? Spit it out. Even a college girl like you can do it."

"Well, since you graduated from a university, I'll use small words. Hmm, I'm thinking of a four-letter word that rhymes with hazy."

The door swung open. Grey stood there in her princess nightie holding her teddy bear.

Leslie called out to her. "Morning, Grey. I'm going to make waffles for you. Hungry?"

"Sure. Where's Abs?"

"She and Rachel went for a walk."

"Can I go find them?"

Connor walked over and picked her up. "They'll be back in a few minutes. Why don't you take your shower and when you get out, I bet they'll be back." He kissed her cheek.

She wriggled loose. "Okay. Can you put blueberries in the waffles, Aunt Leslie?"

His sister laughed. "Sure, sweetie."

Grey ran out of the swinging door. Connor shook his head. "She's something, isn't she?"

"Connor?" He turned to face his sister. She was no longer smiling. "I had a long talk with Lisa last night."

"How is the newlywed?"

"Happy, I guess. She and her new hubby both want a completely fresh start."

"That's why they moved to Bakersfield, right?"

"I guess, but she asked a gigantic favor, and this floored me." She touched his arm, her hand still sticky from the filling. "I'll need your help with this."

The way her hand trembled bothered him. He wiped the sticky bread mixture from his arm. *Leslie's worried?* "Say the word and it's yours."

"She asked if I would consider adopting Grey. Permanently."

***

Backing through the swinging door, Aubrey held it open for Grey. The girl's hands held the homemade cranberry relish the two of them had made while Aubrey carried the mashed potatoes.

When it seemed the table could hold no more, everyone sat down. Connor was on her right and Grey sat on her left. Rachel was across the table, between Mimes and Leslie. Aubrey's mind drifted back to the Thanksgiving she and Rachel had shared last year. Old movies and Chinese takeout were the whole of it. Aubrey couldn't help but smile at the bounty around the table, and she wasn't only thinking about the food.

Connor squeezed her hand. "Rachel, Aubrey, our custom at Thanksgiving is for each of us to say a few words about our blessings. You don't have to, but I didn't want you to be caught unaware. I'll begin." His words were eloquent, expressing thanks for so many blessings, then talking about each person by name. He waited until he was almost finished before mentioning Aubrey. "And certainly not to be last, I want to thank You for bringing Aubrey, this beautiful and vibrant woman into our lives. And I'm ever grateful that she was there to save my life, and give me a second chance to live."

"Thanks for Abs," Grey began her turn. "For her playing games with me and taking me for walks. For being my bestest friend, ever. Love you, Abs."

Aubrey was deeply touched. Finally her turn. *How do I express this?* "This is the favorite time in my life. I'm surrounded by people who only want me to be happy and included. I was so skeptical when Rachel sent me here, to a place foreign to me. In the company of strangers so different than anyone I've ever known. But they are no longer strangers, they've become what I've always wanted. A family, my family. I've changed and become a new person. And my heart is full of thanksgiving for this."

While the food was delightful, the conversation and warmth of love around the table filled her heart.

Touching her chin and turning it so she faced him, Connor winked. "Do you like our traditions?" His blue eyes smiled at her.

"Um-hmm."

He addressed his sister, but continued to hold Aubrey's attention. "Should we tell her about our after-Thanksgiving tradition?"

Leslie giggled. "I was wondering if you were going to say something."

What's going on? "I'm all ears."

He winked and she read his mind. It wasn't just her ears he was interested in. Connor diverted his gaze momentarily to Leslie. He seemed to be trying to hold back a laugh. "So we feel like family to you, huh?"

Something was up. That was plain to see. "Yes. For the first time, I really feel like I'm part of one."

The corners of his mouth crinkled. "Great. Since you feel that way, I need to tell you one of our oldest family traditions, going back as long as I can remember."

"Enlighten me."

He blurted it out, quickly. "Newest member has to do the Thanksgiving dishes, all by themselves."

Grey yanked on her arm. "Nuh-uh. Don't listen to him. Uncle Connie tries to pull that one on me every year."

Aubrey turned to face him, looking for something pointed to say. He beat her to it. "Just kidding. I seriously was kind of hoping to start a new family tradition tonight. I have reservations for all of us to go to Longwood Gardens. They're decorated for Christmas. Would you go with me, uh, I mean us?"

The glow in those blue eyes melted her heart. "I'd love that."

His hand was warm when he touched her cheek. "Great. Reservations are for six-thirty. Gives you just enough time to do the dishes."

Of course, it wasn't true. Everyone helped. Before she knew it, they were in the parking lot of the gardens. Mimes had declined the offer to come, so it was just the five of them. Though together, Rachel and Leslie paired off while Grey joined Connor and Aubrey. They strolled along the paths, all entranced by the decorations. The weather had changed drastically since the morning. A cold front had lowered the temperature. Aubrey shivered slightly and Connor must have sensed it. He wrapped his arm around her.

Connor led them to the Conservatory, which was lush with eye-popping flowers and a small waterway. Poinsettias seemed to be in abundance. In front of the water feature, Leslie snapped a photo of the three of them. Grey, of course, was in between them.

Leslie motioned to the girl. "Come over here. I want to get a picture of just Aubrey and Connor."

Aubrey dug out her phone and handed it to Grey. "Would you mind taking one for me?"

They posed and turned toward each other. Aubrey's hand was against his chest, his arm at her waist. "Do you like our new tradition?"

She nodded slightly. "Will we do this every year?"

A warm glow was simmering in the blue of his eyes. "I hope this is the first of many traditions we'll make, meaning you and me." He drew her closer. "Can I tell you something?"

"Yes, please do."

His face turned bright red. "This isn't just something new, what's inside of me. I've felt this way since our chance meeting on the train." He hesitated, piquing her interest even further.

"What's that?"

Connor's fingers touched her chin, drawing her lips close to his. "I want a life with you. Not just as friends, but so much more." He swallowed hard. "I love you, Aubrey, and I'm hoping someday you'll be my wife."

It became hard to breathe. "Is this a proposal?"

Connor rubbed his nose against hers. "Not yet. Let's say it's a coming-out event." He moved back slightly to gaze into her eyes. "What do you think? Would you like that?"

Moment of truth. "That day on the train, after it was over. When you stood on the stairs looking back at me, I felt the exact same thing. In my heart, I willed you to come running back and kiss me. I wished we could head off into the sunset, and spend every single minute of our lives together."

He'd never smiled as wide. Without a word, his lips found hers. Words were no longer needed. The feelings in their hearts came through, loud and clear.

When they finally pulled apart, the other three were there. Grey was all smiles, too. Handing Aubrey her phone, she laughed. "I got it, Abs."

Rachel twittered and winked. "We all did."

Chapter 19

Standing at the front door, Connor was having a hard time saying goodbye. Aubrey kissed him again, long and soft before making sure his jacket was zipped up the whole way. He lifted her chin so their eyes could meet. "I'm going to miss you today."

"I'll be right here, waiting for you when you get back."

"Promise?"

"Cross my heart."

He kissed her fingers. "I wish you would come with me."

"You know Monday is invoice day. I have to send out the bills, plus I need to order new plumbing fixtures for the Enola job, schedule contractors..."

"Fine, I can see where I'm not wanted."

She grabbed his face and kissed him again. "You know that's not true. If I could have my way, we'd never be apart."

"I love you, Aubrey."

Her eyes sparkled. "I love you, too."

Connor gave her another deep hug, then left. It was very cold this morning and he had to scrape frost off the windows. Backing out onto the road, he caught a glimpse of her figure standing at the door.

Waving, Connor honked his horn and blew her a kiss as he passed. Next, he depressed the phone button on the steering wheel and called out his command.

The woman's voice reflected annoyance. "Took you long enough. I was beginning to wonder if you'd call. What, were you two making out, again?"

"It's hard leaving Aubrey. Even harder trying to keep our secret from her. We still on for lunch?"

"Uh-huh. Do you thing she suspects anything?"

"Nope, she doesn't have a clue. I appreciate you doing this for me. And you're sure you know what size?"

"Why do you even doubt me?"

Connor shook his head. "Because you're my sister. How'd you get the ring size?"

"Oh, I have my ways."

"Is this one of those women things again?"

She laughed. "No. When Aubrey and Grey were painting each other's fingernails the other night, I stuck Aubrey's ring in my therapy dough. Gotta tell you though, it was touch and go. She almost caught me. The jeweler will be able to get her size from the impression."

"I need to watch you. You're sneaky. Wise, but sneaky."

"I have to be smart. Remember, I got stuck with you as a brother."

Connor smiled. "You think I'm going too fast?"

"Not at all. I'm just sorry I won't be there to see you ask her. Tell me again why you are taking her to New York to propose."

"Because Aubrey confided in me how each year, she would go to the Rockefeller tree on Christmas

Eve. She'd fantasize the man of her dreams would suddenly appear, kneel down and propose."

"Aww. How romantic. Too bad she'll be stuck with you." Leslie giggled. "Seriously, that's so sweet. But when you get married, I want a paragraph in the wedding bulletin giving me the credit for bringing you two together. For months, I've watched you both try to avoid the fact you were made for each other. Good thing I got sick when I did, so Aubrey had to go along and spend the long weekend with you. And that whole thing about eating shrimp and almost dying, that was a nice touch."

Connor took a long sip of the coffee Aubrey had prepared for him. He ignored his sister's jabs. "Winning her heart was worth almost dying. Oh, I forgot to ask. Have you considered Lisa's proposal?"

"About adopting Grey?"

"Yep."

"I did, but I'm going to need your help. Maybe the two of you should adopt her. You know, one of these days, I'm going to get serious about finding the right man. I've put it off while I grew the business and was just too busy. But now that Aubrey's here, for the first time I actually have a few minutes to myself."

"You know we'll help."

"We?"

"We—as in Aubrey and I. Or is there bad cell reception?"

"Why Connor, you're talking like an old married guy. Don't count your chickens before they're hatched."

"I'm not. That's why I need to get that engagement ring on her finger."

Leslie laughed at him. "And like usual, your older sister will help you out. See you at the jewelry store at lunch."

After disconnecting, his mind wandered. *Will she say yes?* He'd find out on Christmas Eve.

***

Aubrey punched in Rachel's number. Tingly feelings ran down her arms as she waited for her friend to answer. The air was scented with the fresh fragrance of pine from the tree. The one she and *her* family had decorated together.

Rachel finally picked up. "Hey Abs, what's up?"

"Hope I'm not bothering you. You still on your commute?"

"Uh-huh. A couple of stops before I get there. How's the dairy princess today?"

"You told me to keep you in the loop, so..."

Rachel's voice was suddenly filled with excitement. "Spill the beans. It's so hard keeping up with you. What happened now?"

"Grey and I were painting each other's nails a couple days ago. I took off my rings, but when I went to put them back on, one was missing. I thought maybe I was mistaken, but it reappeared like twenty minutes later."

"Why do you think..." Aubrey could almost feel the sudden rush of air from Rachel's breath. "Good heavens! Connor took it for ring sizing?"

Aubrey was having trouble keeping her joy inside. "That's what I'm thinking, especially since that's the one I wear on my ring finger. Then, he asked me if he could take me somewhere special on Christmas Eve."

"Where?"

"He said it was a surprise, but I do believe Connor forgot he gave me access to his work email so I could monitor it for him. He made hotel reservations and purchased two train tickets to... guess where."

"I don't know."

"Remember when I shared my dreams with you? About my romantic Christmas fantasy?"

"The one with the Rockefeller tree? You told him about that?"

"I did and he's purchased two tickets to New York City on Christmas Eve. Maybe I've worked my hopes up too high, but..."

There was background noise that sounded like a bus braking. "I'm so happy for you. Envious, but happy. Gotta go. This is my stop."

"Bye, Rach."

"Have a great day, Abs."

Aubrey sat back in the recliner. She hadn't had time to tell her friend the other news, what she'd seen when she was on her walk this morning. About the charming old farmette just down the road with a "for sale" sign that hadn't been there yesterday.

Closing her eyes, the vision of Connor's face was before her. Aubrey dreamed out loud. "What would you think of us buying that place? Of making it our own, a home for you and me... and our children someday? We can raise chickens and cows and—"

A loud rap on the door interrupted the fantasy. Aubrey danced over and swung it open. Her mouth went dry when she recognized who was standing there.

"Good morning, Aubrey."

"What do you want?"

"My, my. That certainly isn't the most pleasant way to greet a guest." Marci strolled past her and then sat in the recliner Aubrey had just vacated. "We need to chat."

Aubrey's eyes narrowed. "There's nothing I have to say to you. I want you to leave."

Marci smiled, quite pleasantly. "I will, in a little while. So, I did a little research on you. And I'm impressed. You're a great actress, playing the part of a sweet innocent girl, when deep inside you're a violent woman with a jaded past."

It was suddenly cold in the room. "What's that supposed to mean?"

"And the way you've bonded with that dear sweet child... You know Grey thinks highly of you. She even told Dirk she wishes you were her mother."

"Dirk?"

Marci crossed her legs and clasped her hands over her knees. "Did you know he and I graduated from high school together? I help him out from time to time, in exchange for information and occasional comfort. I know all about you, Aubrey. How you worked your way into this family. Gave Grey hope she'll have a normal childhood, with you in it, of course. But all that is about to change."

Aubrey's hands were shaking. "What do you mean, about to change?"

Marci laughed in a wicked way that creeped Aubrey out. "What do you think Connor and Leslie will do when I tell them the truth about you? That this goody two shoes, the woman they invited to live with them, has a violent and slutty history. When they discover the truth, they'll kick you to the curb quicker than red wine stains white carpet."

"Violent and... did you say slutty? What is that supposed to mean?"

Marci rubbed her hands together. The expression on her face was like a child who'd just opened a wonderful birthday present. "It takes a special kind of person to have a warrant placed for her arrest. Even I was surprised. Aubrey Stettinger, wanted for attempted murder—at eighteen, don't you think?"

Aubrey's blood ran cold. "Attempted murder?"

Marci smiled like a politician who was just re-elected. "That's the charges your real family filed against you. And oh, by the way, your step-brother Roger is dying to know where you are. He can't wait for you to see your handiwork. You know, what you did to his face. Quite horrifying, even after all these years."

The vision of that terrible morning came back. Aubrey had been in the kitchen, frying bacon when Roger suddenly appeared and groped her from behind. He had been very drunk. Roger had forced her against the counter, trying to kiss her. *"For years, you been teasing me. With that long hair and lipstick. I can't hold back no more. I gonna have you, girl."*

"Leave me alone. Help!"

"No one's in the house, but you and me. Don't fight and I won't have to hurt you. One way or another, it's gonna happen."

Aubrey had slapped him. He had grabbed her shirt, ripped it open and lifted her onto the counter. Roger pulled her hair and tried to force her against the wall. Aubrey reached for the first weapon she could find, the frying pan. She threw the hot bacon grease on his face. When he fell to the floor, screaming, she ran to her room, packed her essentials and took off. That was the day she hitchhiked to St. Paul and later caught a bus to New York City. And Aubrey had never looked behind.

Marci's words brought her back to the present. "Nothing to say for yourself?"

"I acted in self-defense."

"Roger doesn't think so. He harbors a grudge against you. In fact he offered me quite a bit of money to tell him where you live."

"You... you didn't, did you?"

"Not yet. I'll keep that in my back pocket, for now. But I don't think I'll need it. You see, when I tell the Lapps that you were a prostitute, I'm sure they'll run you out of town themselves. They're good people and will do anything to protect Grey. Especially if they want to move forward and adopt that little girl."

The anger flowing through Aubrey's body was enough to make her want to slap this witch. "A prostitute? I never did any such thing."

Marci retrieved a manila envelope from her bag and tossed it at her. "I'm sure Connor won't be happy when he sees this. Will he, Aubrey Lynne?"

Aubrey Lynne? That was the name the manager told her to use when answering the phone. Her hands were trembling as she opened the envelope. It was her face on the photo, but the rest from the neck down wasn't her. Emblazoned across the top was her "work name" and the logo of the company where she'd been employed. "I worked for this company, but this, this picture... it's not me."

"Sure looks like a younger version of you."

"Well, yes, the face is me, but not the rest of it. I would never let anyone take those kinds of pictures of me."

"Come on, Aubrey. The escort company you worked for provided young women to satisfy men's needs."

"No. Not that way. We provided companionship, nothing more."

"Escort is just a fancy name for a hooker."

"No, it's not. And besides, I only answered the phones and made appointments. I never left the office. Only worked there for three weeks."

"Was that before or after the naked pictures of you appeared on the internet?"

How does she know all of this? "S-someone stole my phone and posted them. They were private pictures."

Marci laughed. "You walk around with naked pictures of yourself on your cell?"

"No, no! I fell off the stage. I had to take those pictures to show how badly I was injured, for the insurance company. And it was only from behind. You have to believe me, Marci."

"Slant it however you want. It doesn't matter to me. What we're both concerned with is how the Lapps will take it." She threw a thick sheaf of papers on Aubrey's lap. "Wait until they read the results of the investigation I had done into your past. It's amazing what a good private detective can discover."

Aubrey rifled through the report. "This is a lie. These are only half-truths."

Marci pointed at it. "So you say, yet it's all there in black and white. And the report is from a highly respected private investigation firm. What do you think the Lapps will say? We both know how important that child is to them."

"No, please don't do this to me. Have a heart. Marci, please. For the first time in my life, I'm happy."

Marci stood, towering over her. "Poor little Aubrey. You know, there is one thing that could make this go away."

"What's that?"

The red-headed woman's eyes narrowed. "Leave. Now."

Aubrey's whole body was trembling. She stood and faced Marci. "No. This is where I belong."

Marci shoved her back into the chair. "No. This is where *I* belong. Everything you have was once mine before you stole it. But rest assured, the queen will get everything back that's rightfully hers. And I'm fully prepared to make sure you pay the full price, if you resist. I'll make sure they never get Grey. In fact, maybe *I'll* adopt her. The choice is yours. I'm coming over tonight and if you're still here, I'll give this packet to the Lapps. I can guarantee their reaction won't be good—for you. Just think of how tragic the ordeal will be for poor Grey, to see her beloved Abs kicked to the curb in front of her. And then there's the subject of Roger. He can't wait to find out where you are."

Aubrey fought back a sob. "You're a horrible person, Marci. Why do you hate me so much?"

Marci's expression changed. The sinister smile cut Aubrey deeply. "Since the second you appeared on that train, you were trying to take Connor from me, but I don't give up easily. So you and I, we danced. You might have won the early battles, however, it wasn't total victory. But this? It's called checkmate."

Marci turned and walked to the door. She opened it, her profile blocking out the sunshine. "Good riddance, Aubrey. If you're still here tonight, I will publicly destroy you. I can guarantee you'll wish you were never born. Good riddance." The slamming of the door was like an exclamation point.

Chapter 20

Lost in a wonderful daydream, Connor's mind wasn't fully on the road. He could feel the happiness from his vision. On his knee, in front of the big Rockefeller tree. And despite all the people around, he only saw Aubrey. She'd once told him how every year, she would come to the tree on Christmas Eve and dream about her true love asking her to marry him. The wonder in her eye, the beauty of her face. Her breath, captured in chilly vapor as she watched the man of her dreams.

The ring of the phone interrupted his thoughts. *Leslie's ringtone.* "Hey, sis."

Something in her voice raised the hair on the back of Connor's neck. "Is Aubrey with you?"

"No, why?"

"Have you talked to her lately?"

"Not since this morning. I called a couple of times, but she must have been busy. Why?"

"Connor, the house has been ransacked. And Aubrey's gone."

He almost swerved off the road. "What?"

"All our work files are strewn everywhere. The laptops are missing. The kitchen's been trashed. Many of my antiques are gone. And Aubrey's room has been cleaned out. She's not here."

Connor exited the interstate, turned around and headed home. His afternoon appointments would have to wait. "I don't understand."

"Me neither. My first impression is that Aubrey ripped us off and then left." His sister hesitated. "But I'm having a hard time believing it. That's not who I thought she was. Connor, I'm scared."

"Call the police, then wait outside. I'm on my way home."

"I didn't mean for me. I'm thinking about Grey. You know how much the girl loves Aubrey. This will destroy her."

It was a struggle to control his breath. "I don't know what happened or why. We'll figure it out together. I'll be there as soon as I can. I'm going to try and reach her. Now, hang up and call 911."

Connor immediately dialed Aubrey. It went directly to voicemail. "Aubrey, call me. I'm worried about you and don't understand what happened. Need to know you're safe. I love you, Aubrey."

God, please wrap your arms around her and keep Aubrey safe. Help Leslie, too... His prayer was interrupted by the blaring siren and flashing lights from behind his truck. Glancing at his speedometer, he knew why. The needle was just above ninety. *Marvelous, just marvelous.*

***

Not one, but two police cruisers were sitting in front of the house, lights flashing. Connor parked and ran onto the porch. Opening the door, he couldn't believe his eyes. *Why would someone do this?*

"Connor?" Leslie reached for him. "I'm so glad you're here."

He held her. "Where else would I be at a time like this? Are you okay?"

"As good as can be expected, I guess. Can you believe this happened?"

"No. I tried to reach Aubrey, but the calls just go to voicemail."

A police officer walked over, holding a piece of paper. He eyed Connor. "Who are you?"

"Connor Lapp. I live here with my sister."

The man turned his eyes back to Leslie. "We found this." He handed her a printed sheet. Connor and Leslie read it silently.

Leslie,

Thanks for your help, but it's time for me to move on. I needed some money to start over, so I'm sure you'll understand why I took the computers. Someday, when I'm able to, I'll repay you.

Connor,

Sorry I led you on, but we both know this wouldn't have worked. You're better off without me. If you really knew who I was, you would understand. Never try to contact me again.
Goodbye,
Aubrey

Leslie shook her head. "This doesn't make sense." She turned to the officer. "Aubrey knew where I kept my cash and my valuable jewelry, but those weren't touched. If she wanted money, like the note says, there it was. But to take the office computers and leave this mess? Why?"

"Was there something of value on the missing devices? Account numbers, financial information?"

Leslie caught Connor's eye. "Of course there was, but she had access to all that information, every day. We trusted her."

The second policeman approached. He held a manila envelope in his hand. "What was the woman's name, again?"

Leslie beat Connor to the reply. "Aubrey. Aubrey Stettinger."

"Was her middle name Lynne?"

Leslie turned to Connor. He answered. "No. It's Grace."

The officer pulled a piece of paper partially from the packet and displayed a photo. A much younger version of Aubrey was smiling at them. "Is this her?"

Leslie tilted her head as she faced the officer. "Where'd you get that?"

"It was tucked under the pillow. She must have kept it there."

"May I take a closer look?"

The man handed it to her. Leslie removed the page from the covering. Her eyes grew large and her face turned beet red. "Why would she... I mean, Grey was in her room all the time. And to think... This is unbelievable. Guess we didn't know her at all."

Connor grabbed the item from her hand. He quickly turned it over and handed it back to the policeman. *Aubrey?* Having a picture like that where Grey might find it? *No. This wasn't Aubrey.*

Leslie's brows were furrowed. "What kind of a woman did we allow in our home?"

The feeling struck him like a shock wave. "Wait. This is familiar. I've seen this before."

Leslie appeared confused. "Seen what? This photo?"

"No." Connor ran up the stairs and threw open the door to his bedroom. He studied the books on his shelf momentarily before grabbing a hardcover copy. He leafed through it as he returned. "I've read this exact detail before. In *The Lamb and the Wolf.*"

Leslie was waiting at the bottom of the stairs. "I... I don't get it."

"The story line and plot. From one of Marci's novels. It went down exactly like this, where the villain set up the heroine to destroy her credibility."

Now the officer was shaking his head. "Wait, I'm confused. What's a book have to do with the robbery?"

Connor held the novel up for everyone to see. "What happened today, it's already been written. By my ex-girlfriend. In the book, the setup drove the heroine away."

"What happens next in the book?"

Connor shook his head and then swallowed hard. "We can't let that happen."

***

Aubrey slipped the key in the lock and shoved the door open. The décor was something out of the '90s. Stale cigarette smoke permeated everything. She dropped her duffle to the floor and crawled onto the bed. The anger and sadness she'd held inside since the morning finally boiled over. *How could Marci be so mean?* Aubrey had no choice but to leave.

When her sobs finally subsided, she retrieved her phone from the bag and then turned it on. Dozens of missed calls—from Connor. *I let you down.* She deleted his messages without listening to them. Suddenly, the device rang in her hand. *Rachel.*

"Hello?"

"Aubrey, thank God. I just got this frantic call from Leslie. Are you alright?"

She palmed her eyes. "No."

"What happened?"

"My world ended. Every hope, every dream, shattered beyond repair."

"I don't understand. Leslie told me their house had been ransacked. The work computers are missing, and so are you."

"Ransacked? What do you mean?"

"Their home was trashed. Leslie said the police want to talk to you."

Finally, she understood the completeness of Marci's plan. Aubrey's life was in ruins.

"You need to talk to them. To help straighten this out. You owe it to Leslie."

A roach ran along the molding of the floor. "I... I c-can't do that, Rach."

"What? After all they've done for you?"

What Aubrey needed to do was painfully clear. "You've been a great friend and I'm going to miss you. Please tell Leslie I didn't do it. I'd never betray her. When you speak to Connor, let him know I'll always love him... and that I'm sorry. Tell Grey I wish her happiness and I'll never forget her."

"Aubrey, stop it. What is going on with you? Why don't you just call the police and explain what happened?"

Aubrey wiped her sleeve across her face. "I'm not going to talk to the police. You've been a great friend, but this," she fought back a sob, "this is goodbye."

Before Rachel could say anything, Aubrey disconnected. She immediately blocked her friend's number, as well as Leslie's. She pulled up Connor's contact. His photo, the one linked to his contact, stared back at her. Those deep blue eyes, that smile.

Aubrey pressed her lips to the screen. "Goodbye, Connor. I'll always love you." She blocked his number as well and threw her cell on the floor.

Her vision was blurry as she huddled beneath the covers.

"You won, Marci. I give up."

Chapter 21

"Look, the freezing rain's changed to snow. Isn't it beautiful?"

Aubrey nodded at her co-worker as they left the restaurant where they worked. The changing weather was making her legs ache, right where they'd been broken. "Yeah. Guess we'll have a white Christmas after all."

"Want to go out for a drink somewhere, or are you heading home? Maybe waiting for Santa to come, huh?"

Home? I don't have one anymore. "I think I want to walk around the city for a little while." *One last time before I go.* "Christmas Eve, you know? Catch you later."

"Sure thing. Hey, why don't you stop over at my apartment later? Maybe we can watch a movie or something."

Aubrey nodded at her. "Maybe. I'll see, if it's not too late. Merry Christmas."

After the woman left, Aubrey headed east from Times Square. The snowflakes now littering the streets were large, maybe quarter sized. But Aubrey didn't really see them. All she saw were the faces of the people she loved most—Leslie, Grey, Mimes, Rachel and especially Connor. *My family.* Walking ahead of her was another family, one with a girl about Grey's age. *I let them down, all of them.* But at least Leslie and Connor would be able to adopt Grey. *Since I'm out of the picture.*

The scent of roasted chestnuts mixed with the odor of trash along the curb. The snowflakes were cold against her face. Aubrey's mind drifted back to her days in Lancaster. The long talks with Connor. Baking cookies with Grey. Shopping with Leslie. Such happy times. *I'd give anything if the circumstances were different.* But they weren't. When she'd boarded the train in Lancaster, she'd left it all behind. And what she'd left in Pennsylvania was everything—and everyone—she'd ever loved.

Chills ran up her spine when a woman's voice caught her attention. *Marci?* She quickly turned to face her, but it wasn't her nemesis. Instead, it was the mother of the family she'd been following. Despite the late hour, the streets were still crowded, because it was Christmas Eve. Hundreds of people waited to cross the street. The marquee of Radio City Music Hall lit both Sixth Avenue and 50th Street.

Aubrey's eyes were blurry as her feet led her to Rockefeller Plaza. *One last view of the tree I love.* She'd decided to move to Orlando after New Year's Day. To make a fresh start. Time to say goodbye to her dreams. The romantic fantasy she'd always dreamed about would never come true. No matter how much she wished...

Aubrey bumped into the little girl in front of her. "Sorry, honey."

The girl's smile was ear to ear. "Did you see the tree?"

Aubrey's gaze gravitated to the beauty of the evergreen that towered before her. She nodded and answered the child. "It's magical, isn't it?"

But the child was no longer paying attention to her. Her mother was taking a selfie of the three of them with the tree in the background. Aubrey found a place to lean against the GE building. A place to rest her sore legs. The falling snow made it appear as if the lights were twinkling. *Connor, I wanted to share this moment with you. Share all my life with you.* But that dream was gone. She shivered in the cold night air. Laughter and happiness surrounded her, but all Aubrey could feel was the emptiness of her broken heart.

A spoken word disturbed her thoughts. She thought she'd heard a girl's voice call her name, but that was impossible. Her eyes returned to the twinkling lights. *You sent your Son on a cold Christmas Eve long ago. Please bless and bring happiness to Grey and...*

A warm touch against her hand startled her. Fingers wound themselves in hers. She whipped around to face the person who was invading her personal space. Her mouth fell open. *Connor?*

His smile was like a brilliant sunrise after the darkest night. "Knew I'd find you here."

Her breath all but refused to come out. "Why are you here?"

Aubrey realized he was holding both of her hands. "You know why."

A horrid thought took hold in the pit of her stomach. *He's here to take me in, for his house being ransacked.* "But I... I, uh, you've got to believe me.

Rachel told me what happened to your home. I didn't do it."

The lights of the tree were reflected in his blue eyes. "Never once suspected that you did."

"Then why are you in New York City?"

Was that merriment in his eyes? "Oh, for a couple of reasons."

"Such as?"

"My first priority was to find you."

Hope was rising inside, but it was bittersweet. A life between the two of them was now impossible. "I don't understand."

His palm was warm against her cheek. "This city's not your home anymore. I miss you. Your family misses you. Aubrey, you belong in Paradise. It's time to come home."

"Connor..."

"We both know that's where you're wanted, and needed. I came to take you there."

A knife through her heart wouldn't have hurt as badly. "I can't go back to Lancaster."

He moved closer, lips mere millimeters away. "Why?"

Aubrey shrank closer to the building. "I just can't." She could feel a warm liquid on her cheek.

He gently wiped her tears away. "If it had anything to do with the lies Marci fed you, you needn't worry about them, or her anymore. Marci will never bother you again. I'm here to protect you from her, or anyone else. And that's a promise I will always keep."

"H-how did you know about Marci?"

"Grey's dad told us. Seems the police caught him red-handed with the things that were stolen from Leslie's house. He confessed that Marci put him up to it. She wasn't so tough when the police interrogated her. Marci spilled her guts about what she tried to do to you. Trying to scare you away. Threatening that if you stayed, we couldn't adopt Grey. Bold faced lies, Aubrey."

"I couldn't risk that little girl's happiness."

"I know. But that's not the case anymore. We want you to come back. *I* want you to come home... with me. Please?"

Aubrey's head was spinning. "Is this real or am I hallucinating?"

Connor kissed her hand. "Nope. And you're not imagining this, either." Her eyes flew open wide when Connor dropped to one knee, pulling a small box from his pocket. He flipped it open. The lights from the tree reflected brilliantly in the stone. "Aubrey Grace Stettinger, I love you. Have since the second I caught a glimpse of you on that train. Beyond any reasonable doubt, God brought us together. And neither of us can deny we belong together. And know this one thing—you, Aubrey, are the love of my life and I will love you and only you until my dying day. Will you marry me?"

Her body shuddered as she closed her eyes. *This must be a cruel nightmare.* She knew when she opened them again, Connor would be gone. *God, I trusted you. Why are you allowing my mind to torture me?* Her brain was only playing a nasty trick on her.

Taking a deep breath, Aubrey forced her eyelids to open. She was totally unprepared for the sight that greeted her.

Epilogue

T he kitchen was filled with wonderful traces of cinnamon, pine and fresh baked cookies. Aubrey glanced out the window, awe-struck by the beauty of the falling snow covering the Hemlock trees in the backyard. The kitchen timer tugged her attention away from the breathtaking landscape. The perfectly browned chocolate chip cookies looked plump and moist. *Last batch.*

The door swung open and two snow-covered figures tumbled in, laughing. Aubrey turned just in time to duck the snowball Connor tossed at her. With a look she hoped was the opposite of the joy in her heart, she admonished him. "Connor Lapp. You clean that up, this second."

He winked at her. "Yes, dear."

Grey slid across the kitchen floor, reached for Aubrey and then gave her a warm hug. Aubrey knew it was coming and acted surprised when the girl stuck a handful of snow down the back of her shirt. Before Aubrey could react, Grey kissed her cheek. The words the girl spoke pulled at her heartstrings. "Love you, Momma." Only last week, Grey had quit calling her "Abs" and now referred to her exclusively as "Momma."

"You two are just in time. The last batch of cookies just came out of the oven. Ready for some cold milk and warm cookies?"

They both nodded. Connor's blue eyes were twinkling. "I have the sleigh ready to go for later. I'll just need to hitch up the horses. Anything I can help with to prepare for the party?"

"After our snack, both of you could help me get the presents under the tree."

Grey's words were choppy because they came in between chomps of cookies. "Can I open a present?"

Aubrey glanced at Connor. He nodded his head and shot her a wink. "Yes, you may. Uncle Connie and I have a special gift we want you to open before everyone gets here. I'll go get it."

Aubrey pushed back her chair and ran upstairs to the room she and Connor shared. Warmth filled her heart as she pulled the gift from her dresser drawer. Aubrey glanced in the mirror. The reflection smiling back at her revealed a happy woman so different than she'd felt exactly one year ago. *Thank you, Lord, for my many blessings and making all my dreams come true.* She held the special gift close to her heart for a second before heading back down the stairs. As she descended, the house phone rang.

Connor had answered, but she caught the look of surprise in his eyes. "Sure, here she is now. Just hold on." He covered the mouthpiece and handed her the phone. "Aubrey, there's a man asking for you. He said his name is Roger. Claims he's your brother."

Chills filled her body. *Roger?* The last she'd talked to or seen him had been that day in the kitchen, when he tried to accost her. Hesitating, she looked to Connor for support. He gripped her hand. "I'll be right here."

Aubrey nodded and placed the receiver to her ear. "Hello?"

"Hi. Are you Aubrey Stettinger, the one who lived in Benson, Minnesota, with a preacher step-father and his four unruly sons?"

"I'm Aubrey Lapp now, but yes. And you are?"

She had to pull the phone away when the man hollered into the phone. "Aubrey. Hi, this is Roger, your step-brother. How are you?"

"I-I-I'm well, and you?"

"We're all doing great." His voice grew quieter. "I remember the last day I saw you, and what I said to you. I wish I could undo it. Please forgive me. I was drunk. Can you excuse what I did?"

Aubrey's mouth fell open. "Of course. Can you pardon me for throwing hot oil on you?"

The man was laughing. "Nothing to forgive. I deserved it. Aubrey, my brothers and their families are with me. The four of us have been talking about looking for you since Dad passed away. Our family's just not complete without our little sister. Some guy came around late last year, asking questions about you and that got us thinking that maybe we should reach out. We want to wish you a Merry Christmas. Can I put you on speaker phone?"

They spoke for almost half an hour before hanging up. She turned to Connor and Grey, who had completely consumed the cookies she'd just baked. "They asked me to visit them after the holidays. Would the two of you like to tag along?"

Connor winked. "Wouldn't miss it for the world."

Grey pulled at her arm. "Can I open my present now?"

Aubrey caught Connor's smile and nod. "Yes. This is something special." She pulled the small, flat package from her pocket and handed it to the girl.

Grey ripped the paper and exposed the gift. Her eyes grew as large as dinner plates. Grey charged into Aubrey's arms and kissed her. "Thank you, Momma."

***

Connor propped the toboggan against the snowman. "Looks like he's ready to go sledding."

Grey danced around. *Too much sugar from all the cookies she ate.* "That was fun. Can we go tobogganing again when Aunt Leslie and Rach get here?"

Aubrey touched her nose. "We'll see. How about we go in and get warm first? I need to set the food out."

Connor took her hand and motioned down the road toward his sister's house. "I think our guests are on the way." He pointed to three figures walking along the road.

"Rach! Aunt Leslie! Mimes!" Grey took off down the road to greet them.

After a round of hugs, everyone filed into the house. Connor volunteered to make hot chocolate. Rachel stayed in the living room with Aubrey.

"Wow, you two really made a lot of headway on the house. This fireplace, it's new, isn't it?"

"Yep. Connor and I built it ourselves."

Rachel turned to her, mouth hanging open. "You learned how to lay bricks, too? What, are you secretly Super Woman inside?"

Aubrey couldn't help but smile. "I've found you can do anything, if you put your mind to it."

Rachel shook her head as she examined the photos on the mantle. She lifted a frame, from last Christmas Eve. "I remember the look of shock on your face. When you opened your eyes and saw all of us standing there in Rockefeller Center so we could watch the proposal... You know, Connor believed with all his heart you would stop by to see the tree. We waited there all day and night. Grey wanted to see you so badly and she was the one who saw you first. And Connor? His greatest desire was to make your dream come true. And he wanted all of the family to be there to support and share that moment with you. Of course, Leslie told him she needed to be there so he wouldn't mess it up. You do realize that man loves you like crazy, don't you? You're so lucky, Abs."

Not lucky, I'm blessed. "I know. Last Christmas Eve turned from the worst day into the best ever. When I turned and saw his face... It was so hard to believe."

Rachel laughed. "That's what happens when you have true love. So what's new with the dairy princess?"

Aubrey couldn't help but smile. "Remember when I told you about the audition?"

Her friend's eyes grew large. "Yes. You auditioned at a local theater—for the role of Nellie Forbush in *South Pacific*, right?"

Aubrey sat on the rocker. "Um-hmm."

"Did you get it? Don't keep me in suspense!"

"Yes and no."

Rachel shook her head. "What's that mean?"

"They offered me the lead, but I decided to split the role with another actress. I'll be on stage two nights a week. I've got too much going on around here to be a full-time actress."

Her friend hugged her tightly. "I'm so proud of you."

"It's not Broadway, but..."

Grey stuck her head out of the kitchen. "Momma, hot chocolate's ready."

"I'll be there in a few seconds, sweetheart."

Rachel's mouth dropped open. "Momma? She called you Momma. When did this happen?"

"She started calling me that just recently." Aubrey's heart was overflowing with happiness. "I've got something else to tell you."

"What else could there possibly be? You had the proposal you've always wanted, married the man of your dreams, live in a beautiful house the two of you have made into a home, landed a starring role in a musical and now that beautiful little girl calls you Momma. Are you going to tell me you also won the lottery?"

Aubrey moved her head toward the kitchen door. "Come find out."

Soon, all six of them were sitting around the big kitchen table. Aubrey cast a glance at Connor. He was all smiles. She nodded. Connor cleared his throat. "Thank you for coming to our home to celebrate tonight. Lest we forget, the reason for the season is the birth of a child, the first Christmas present." His eyes flitted between the three guests. "The act is about to be repeated, over two thousand years later."

Glancing around the table, Aubrey could see the lights of understanding begin to come on.

Connor continued. "We're blessed to have so much love filling this home. But," he reached for Aubrey's hand, "love is the one thing you can never have too much of." He smiled at Grey. "Sweetheart, can you share your Christmas gift with everyone?"

All eyes turned to the girl. She pulled a pin from her pocket. "I'm gonna be the big sister!"

Leslie was the first one to reach Aubrey. "I'm so happy for you. Are you having a little girl or boy?"

"We don't know, yet."

"If it's a girl, you should name her after me."

Rachel was next. "It looks like you did win the lottery. How did this happen?"

Casting a happy glance at her husband, Aubrey replied, "This was God's plan for me, all along. To have a real family." She reached for Connor's hand and pulled him into her arms. "To find true love. To live the rest of my life, in Paradise."

The End

Other Books by this Author

Seeking Forever (Book 1)

Kaitlin Jenkins long ago gave up the notion of ever finding true love, let alone a soulmate. Jeremy is trying to get his life back on track after a bitter divorce and an earlier than planned departure from the military. They have nothing in common, except their distrust of the opposite sex.

An unexpected turn of events sends these two strangers together on a cross-country journey—a trip fraught with loneliness and unexpected danger. And on this strange voyage, they're forced to rely on each other—if they want to survive. But after the past, is it even possible to trust anyone again?

Seeking Forever is the first book of Chas Williamson's Seeking series, the saga of the Jenkins family over three generations.

Will Kaitlin and Jeremy ever be the same after this treacherous journey?

Seeking Happiness (Book 2)

Kelly was floored when her husband of ten years announced he was leaving her for another woman. But she isn't ready to be an old maid. And she soon discovers there's no shortage of men waiting in line.

Every man has his flaws, but sometimes the most glaring ones are well hidden. And now and then, those faults can force other people to the very edge, to become everything they're not. And when that happens to her, there's only one thing that can save Kelly.

Seeking Happiness is the second book of Chas Williamson's Seeking series, the saga of the Jenkins family over three generations.

Ride along with Kelly on one of the wildest adventures you can imagine.

Seeking Eternity (Book 3)
At eighteen, Nora Thomas fell in love with her soulmate and best friend, Stan Jenkins. But Nora was already engaged to a wonderful man, so reluctantly, Nora told Stan they could only be friends. Stan completely disappeared (well, almost), from her world, from her life, from everywhere but Nora's broken heart.

Ten painful years later, the widow and mother of two was waiting tables when she looked up and found Stan sitting in her section. But she was wearing an engagement ring and Stan, a wedding ring. Can a woman survive when her heart is ripped out a second time?

Seeking Eternity is the third book of Chas Williamson's Seeking series, a glimpse at the beginning of the Jenkins' family saga through three generations.

Will Nora overcome all odds to find eternal happiness?

 **Seeking the Pearl (Book 4)**
Eleanor Lucia has lived a sad and somber life, until she travels to London to open a hotel for her Aunt Kaitlin. For that's where Ellie meets Scotsman Henry Campbell and finally discovers true happiness. All that changes when Ellie disappears without a trace and everyone believes she is dead, well almost everyone.

But Henry and Ellie have a special bond, one that defies explanation. As if she were whispering in his ear, Henry can sense Eleanor begging him to save her. And Henry vows he will search for her, he will find her and he will rescue her, or spend his last breath trying.

Seeking the Pearl is the exciting finale of Chas Williamson's Seeking series, the culmination of the three generation Jenkins' family saga.

Henry frantically races against time to rescue Ellie, but will he be too late?

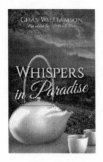

Whispers in Paradise (Book 1)

Ashley Campbell never expected to find love, not after what cancer has done to her body. Until Harry Campbell courts her in a fairy tale romance that exceeds even her wildest dreams. But all that changes in an instant when Harry's youngest brother steals a kiss, and Harry walks in on it.

Just when all her hopes and dreams are within reach, Ashley's world crumbles. Life is too painful to remain in Paradise because Harry's memory taunts her constantly. Yet for a woman who has beaten the odds, defeating cancer not once, but twice, can anything stand in the way of her dreams?

Whispers in Paradise is the first book in Chas Williamson's Paradise series, stories based loosely around the loves and lives of the patrons of Sophie Miller's Essence of Tuscany Tea Room.

Which brother will Ashley choose?

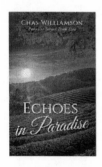

Echoes in Paradise (Book 2)

Hannah Rutledge rips her daughters from their Oklahoma home in the middle of the night to escape a predator from her youth. After months of secrecy and frequent moves to hide her trail, she settles in Paradise and ends up working with Sam Espenshade, twelve years her junior. Sam wins her daughters' hearts, and earns her friendship, but because of her past, can she ever totally trust anyone again?

Yet, for the first time since the death of her husband, Hannah's life is starting to feel normal, and happy, very happy. But a violent attack leaves Sam physically scarred and drives a deep wedge between them. To help heal the wounds, Hannah is forced from her comfort zone and possibly exposes the trail she's tried so hard to cover.

Echoes in Paradise is the second book in Chas Williamson's Paradise series, an exciting love story with Sophie Miller's Essence of Tuscany Tea Room in background.

When the villain's brother shows up on Hannah's doorstep at midnight on Christmas Eve, were the efforts since she left Oklahoma in vain?

Courage in Paradise (Book 3)
Sportscaster Riley Espenshade returns to southcentral Pennsylvania so she can be close to her family while growing her career. One thing Riley didn't anticipate was falling for hockey's greatest superstar, Mickey Campeau, a rough and tall Canadian who always gets what he wants... and that happens to be Riley. Total bliss seems to be at her fingertips, until she discovers Mickey also loves another girl.

The 'other girl' happens to be Molly, a two-year old orphan suffering from a very rare childhood cancer. Meanwhile, Riley's shining career is rising to its zenith when a new sports network interviews her to be the lead anchor. Just when her dream job falls into her lap, Mickey springs his plan on her, a quick marriage, adopting Molly and setting up house.

Courage in Paradise is Chas Williamson's third book in the Paradise series, chronicling the loves and lives of those who frequent Sophie Miller's Essence of Tuscany Tea Room.

Riley is forced to make a decision, but which one will she choose?

Stranded in Paradise (Book 4)

When Aubrey Stettinger is attacked on a train, a tall, handsome stranger comes to her assistance, but disappears just as quickly. Four months later, Aubrey finds herself recuperating in Paradise at the home of a friend of a friend.

When she realizes the host's brother is the hero from the train, she suspects their reunion is more than a coincidence. Slowly, and for the first time in her life, Aubrey begins to trust—in family, in God and in a man. But just when she's ready to let her guard down, life once again reminds her she can't trust anyone. Caught between two worlds, Aubrey must choose between chasing her fleeting dreams and carving out a new life in this strange place.

Stranded in Paradise is the fourth book in the Paradise series, chronicling the loves and lives of those who frequent Sophie Miller's Essence of Tuscany Tea Room.

Will Aubrey remain *Stranded in Paradise*?

Christmas in Paradise (Book 5)
True love never dies, except when it abandons you at the altar.

Rachel Domitar has found the man of her dreams. The church is filled with friends and family, her hair and dress are perfect, and the honeymoon beckons, but one knock at the door is about to change everything.

Leslie Lapp's life is idyllic – she owns her own business and home, and has many friends – but no one special to share her life... until one dark and stormy afternoon when she's forced off the highway. Will the knock at her door be life changing as well?

When love comes knocking at Christmas, will they have the courage to open the door to paradise?

About the Author

Chas Williamson's lifelong dream was to write. He started writing his first book at age eight, but quit after two paragraphs. Yet some dreams never fade...

It's said one should write what one knows best. That left two choices—the world of environmental health and safety... or romance. Chas and his bride have built a fairytale life of love. At her encouragement, he began writing romance. The characters you'll meet in his books are very real to him, and he hopes they'll become just as real to you.

True Love Lasts Forever!

Follow Chas on
www.bookbub.com/authors/chas-williamson

Enjoyed this book?
Please consider placing a review on Amazon!

Made in the USA
Middletown, DE
16 September 2021